Beatrice's Birthday

A fantasy story for all ages

Geoffrey Foster

May 2009

Geoffrey Foster was born in London, England in 1933, and his childhood was mostly spent in the County of Kent, in southeast England. Some of the action of this book, which has occasional echoes of his own experiences, takes place in or around that area, which was semi-rural even when he lived there, and was certainly rural in the Middle Ages, the time of the book.

His father was a policeman most of his working life, and his mother, when she worked, was a shorthand typist (a stenographer). He has two sisters, five and thirteen years younger than himself.

He went to public elementary and secondary school and then to the University of Cambridge, where he studied engineering. Moving to Australia in 1959, he taught Mechanical Engineering at the University of Queensland for 14 years, before switching to educational development, running workshops and other activities for academics. Eventually he took early retirement in 1995.

As well as writing, he likes reading, listening to music, solving cryptic crosswords, walking the family beagle, Kafka, and playing a game with his younger sister, Ynes, that they whimsically refer to as 'tennis.'

Also by Geoffrey Foster and uniform with this volume:

Kit and the Beeman

Kit the Venturer

Vincent the Beeman

ISBN 978-0-9805310-3-9

Chapter 1

It was night-time in Hastings in the Middle Ages, a port town in southern England, and it was early spring and still quite cold, so the streets were mostly empty. If there had been passers-by they might have noticed two suspicious-looking cloaked figures lurking in an alleyway between Master Samuel's silver warehouse and a new shop that was being built next door and was almost completely fitted out and ready to be occupied.

One of these ruffians had just half-heartedly tried the last of the warehouse windows; they had been all around the building, but it had been obvious that great care had been taken to make it secure. There were stout bars at every window, and both front and rear doors were strongly built of oak, studded with iron bolts.

The shorter of the two said "We might of guessed it'd be done up tight, Billy – that old Samuel is a sly bird, and he's been dealing in plate as long as we can remember, me and me pappy both. I reckon we'd do best to wait until they two German women open up this shop o' theirs and start moving stock in; if we're in luck it'll take 'em a while to get sorted and we'll maybe see our chance to pick up a few nice pieces afore they've got settled in properly."

His companion cursed and spat, but had to agree, "Right-oh, Lem, let's get down to the Barbary Inn and see if we can find something to warm our bellies. The talk is that tomorrow is when the shop is going to be stocked; my mate who sometimes works for Hicks the carter thinks that they are bringing some heavy crates up from the docks then. We'd best come back then and hang around and see what's afoot – but let's keep out of sight if we can."

Sure enough, bright and early the next morning, a carriage drew up in front of the shop and two well-dressed middle-aged women got out and unlocked the front door. The taller of the two strode inside and looked around appreciatively, "Well, Clotilda, it seems as though they have been making a good job of the fitting-out; the counters and cabinets look very impressive – I think we were wise to choose rosewood, it will make a nice setting for our sparkling silverware and crystal."

"Yes, Fritzi," replied the other, a rather plump lady with greying hair, "it does look well. Is it really finished and ready for the stock? I believe that our first consignment was due to be unloaded from the ship yesterday, but we haven't had definite word yet, have we?"

"Well, I certainly hope that all will run to time. I would hate to be late for Beatrice's birthday celebrations, so we've only got three days to sort all this out. Mistress Watson, our manageress, told me she couldn't get here until today or tomorrow, and I want to make sure she is well settled in, and the girl, too. I want to know that the shop will be in safe hands and managed properly before we go on to Woodhampton Castle."

The two had a good look round the shop, and the office and storeroom behind, and then climbed the stairs to the apartment above. The manageress and the new saleswoman would live here, and it would also provide a place for the two proprietors to stay whenever they were in Hastings. They had spent the previous night in the Castle Arms, a respectable hotel, not too close to the docks.

The furnishings of the apartment met with their approval, and as they were descending to the shop again, they heard a rumble of wheels on the cobbles outside. Going out, they saw a heavy cart, with several ironbound chests aboard. The driver and a young assistant were just climbing down, and they hailed them. The driver replied. "Good morrow to ye, my ladies, give us a few moments and we'll start unloading. Where do you want these chests put? They're pretty heavy; it be a good job that Perkin here is a strong lad – but we do have a stout barrow with us, so we should manage all right. At the docks there was plenty of willing hands – I did pass out a groat or two, so perhaps you would oblige?"

"I will settle up with you once everything is stowed away," said the one called Fritzi, "there is a door there in the alley that gives on to our storeroom – I'll go through and open it up, it's bolted from the inside."

The carters started to move one of the chests, with much grunting, to the edge of the cart, ready to lower it onto their barrow; and then a couple of rough-looking fellows approached, touched their forelocks, and one said, "Halloo there, master, you look as though you would be glad of some strong arms to help you out. Can me mate Billy and I give you a lift and maybe earn ourselves a drink?"

The driver looked a bit dubious, but then decided to take a chance with them; they looked strong enough. Then Fritzi emerged from the alley and spoke quietly to Clotilda. "I will stay here and watch proceedings, but do you think you could go and see whether Master Samuel can come and watch, too? I would feel a little happier if a man were here; maybe you could ask him to bring a warehouseman with him. I wonder where Mistress Watson has got to – I do hope she will not be too late."

Clotilda went into the warehouse and soon found Samuel, the merchant; he came out readily with a young helper. "Why did you not ask me for hands to help with the unloading?" he said, when he spied the two volunteers. "I can't say I like the look of those two. I know Hicks the carter well enough; he's a sound man and a good worker."

Nevertheless, between the carter's men, the ruffians and the warehouseman, the chests were soon safely locked away in the storeroom and the door barred and bolted. Fritzi gave some coppers to the rough-looking men, who touched their forelocks again and went off whistling, and then she took Hicks into the shop and settled up for the cartage and what he had given out at the docks. As he left, a woman trotted up, red in the face from hurrying, saying "Oh, my lady, I'm sorry I'm late, I've had to leave my valise at the coaching inn; I couldn't find anyone to bring me and my goods here, and my coach only got in just a few minutes ago." It was, of course, Mistress Watson.

Clotilda soothed her, and all three, together with Master Samuel, went into the shop to take a cooling drink, and some cakes, fetched by the young warehouseman, who declined to join them, feeling, Fritzi thought, rather overawed by the ladies and by their German accents.

Fritzi and Clotilda spent the rest of the day discussing with Mistress Watson how to display the goods, and making sure she knew about selling and keeping accounts – they knew she had experience in the trade before.

Satisfied enough, and rather tired after all the day's excitement, they were glad that their carriage had arrived to take them back to the Castle Arms. As they drove off, Clotilda thought she saw the two former helpers, sitting in a doorway on the main street, but she said nothing to Fritzi, not wishing to worry her.

Chapter 2

Woodhampton Castle was in a state of tumult in preparation for the party – servants were running hither and yon; Lord Brendan Musgrave was lecturing Pemberton, the majordomo, on his responsibilities for the arrangements (he had earlier tried this on with Mistress Travis, the housekeeper, but had received short shrift from that formidable personage); Vincent had finished with his beehives for the day, retired to his apartment and was deciding what he should wear that evening and Beatrice was in Lady Louise's sitting room, consoling her mother, who deeply missed her husband at times like this.

"It will take some time, Mama, for your grief to be more manageable" she told her, as she sat beside her on a couch with her arm round her shoulders, "and I will try to help whenever I can. It has only been a year since Papa was taken from us, so nobody feels that you should end your mourning just yet."

Lady Louise smiled through her tears, saying, "Thank you, my dear, it would be much harder for me if it were not for your support and love. And dear Vincent is a tower of strength as well. I am lucky to have such a family! Now, let us attend to our plans – I want this celebration to be happily memorable for all our family and friends for years to come. It is not every day that the daughter of a noble house reaches twenty-five years and attains her majority!"

Just then, a footman knocked at the door and came into the room, saying, with a bow "My lady, I have just been told that Their Majesties' coach and entourage is approaching. The watcher on the battlements judged that they will be at our doors in about ten minutes."

"Thank you, Jobson," said Louise, "Has his lordship been informed? We shall go down to the main hall and welcome them." She dabbed the remaining moisture from her eyes, and hand in hand, she and Beatrice descended the main staircase, to see Brendan already standing there ready, with the majordomo waiting at the doors with his ceremonial staff.

After a few minutes Pemberton ushered King Arnold and Queen Tabitha in, the royal couple acknowledging the bows of their hosts. The majordomo struck three blows of his staff on the floor, saying "Pray silence for his Majesty!"

But the King and Queen waved him to one side, shook Brendan's hand, and embraced Louise and Beatrice. "We thank you most warmly for your invitation!" said King Arnold "We have for too long been putting off our first visit to this fine castle! Since our accession, I fear we have occupied ourselves with matters of state and have neglected our friends. Dear Louise, we have not even consoled you since your spouse passed away. As you know, we were not in this country for the funeral, but nevertheless we should not have left this sad duty until now."

The young Queen Tabitha stepped forward to embrace Louise again and add her greetings and condolences, and then hugged Beatrice once more, saying "I have long thought of you, dear Beatrice, as an older sister, even though we are neither related by blood nor by country of birth. And now, look at you, in the flowering of your maturity you are more beautiful than ever!"

At that moment, Vincent appeared, descending the stairs at a trot, "Please excuse me for not being here to greet you, your majesties both – I needed to change out of my clothes as a humble bee-keeper!" At this, Beatrice, ever quick-witted, said "Why, Vincent, I thought you kept honey bees, not humble bees!"

The King and Queen chuckled at this and embraced Vincent as an old friend.

"Please come and take some light refreshments" invited Louise, "we can then all chat together and relax before the serious feasting commences this evening!"

As they all wandered into the small dining room, Brendan started to ask King Arnold how the old Queen, Miranda, had been finding life over the two years since King Adelbert had passed away. "Well," said King Arnold, "of course, the decisions about succession had all been settled before Adelbert became ill. After all the dreadful business with Prince Godfrey, there were several possibilities, but since there was no-one in the direct line of succession, and since neither Adelbert nor Miranda had brothers or even sisters, they thought it best to look further afield, and to forestall much of the bickering that would have been occasioned between claimants from the

English nobility, they approached the Danish court. Queen Miranda was completely in favour of this, and after Tabitha and I agreed to accept the honour of the throne, she took to us like a sister. She even argued strongly for us when certain elements in the House of Lords looked as though they would raise constitutional difficulties. We have tried to make her comfortable at Winchester and she has her own circle there, of course."

"I asked," said Brendan, "because I have become rather out of touch. My father was a prominent figure at court, of course, but I have never been drawn to that life and visit Winchester only rarely. In fact, my Mama goes there much more than I."

At that point, a footman entered and announced, "The Countess Friederike and Frau Gunther." Fritzi and Clotilda bustled in, smiling and walking around the table, curtseying to the King and Queen, and embracing Louise, Beatrice and Vincent.

Said Fritzi, "We have driven directly from Hastings – we have been supervising the fitting out of our new shop, next door to Master Samuel's warehouse. He has undertaken to keep a general oversight of its operations, but we have engaged a manageress and the first of our sales staff. This is all quite exciting! But I'm a little worried about some men who were taking an undue interest, I thought, as they helped us to move some stock in. I have asked Mr Samuel to keep an eye on them."

"So, it seems that your business is booming," said Louise, "how many establishments have you now?" "Well, the Frankfurt shop is doing quite well," replied Fritzi, "and so is Schloss Kirschbaum, which is our main establishment; we are happily resident in the castle, as you know. Are Ruprecht and Euphemia coming to these celebrations? Or is Ruprecht still away on his honeymoon?"

At this, Beatrice broke into delighted laughter and pointed to the far end of the room, where the shadowy figures of Ruprecht, Euphemia and a slender young woman were slowly materialising. "Does that answer your question?" exclaimed Beatrice, hurrying to greet them.

Ruprecht kissed her and then ushered the stranger forward, saying, "May I introduce my bride, Countess Konstanze of Mittelheim, the new Landgravine of Hesse!"

Chapter 3

After Beatrice, Lady Louise was the first to embrace the new Landgravine, who, seemingly a little nervous, kept her hand in her husband's tender grasp. Louise whispered a few words in her ear, kissing her cheek, whereupon Konstanze blushed charmingly while her blonde curls trembled.

Louise then took her hand from that of the Landgrave, leading her to where the King and Queen were standing and smiling; she curtsied to them and had her hand kissed in reply by King Arnold and was hugged by Queen Tabitha.

Louise then escorted her round to be greeted by all the others, who curtsied or bowed accordingly. Then she stood aside and asked the Countess to say a few words, to which she responded, "Please to excuse me, your Majesties, ladies and gentlemen, I am not yet very good speaker of English; I hope you will be able understand me! I am very happy to come here, and I thank dear Euphemia, and, naturally, my husband Ruprecht, for carrying me here by dreaming in so magical a fashion! And I must congratulate Lady Beatrice on her birthday – we have brought you a gift, Beatrice, should we give it now? What is your English custom?"

Beatrice went to her and embraced her warmly, "By all means, now!" she said, "You will be the first to present me with a gift – but I hope and believe that you will not be the last!"

Konstanze fumbled with the reticule hanging from her wrist and drew out a small black velvet bag, which she handed to Beatrice, kissing her on both cheeks. Beatrice then opened it, exclaiming, "Oh, how I love getting presents! Oh, look, everyone, it is a beautiful jewelled pendant! Please help me, Mama, to fasten it round my neck. Thank you so much, Konstanze!" "And Euphemia and Ruprecht, too!" added the young Landgravine with a smile.

Everyone sat at the table, some merely picking at the dishes, while others, including Fritzi, made a hearty meal. The conversation ranged over many subjects, being enlivened whenever new guests arrived and joined in. Among these was the du Boise family, bringing their instruments with them, for they were to present a musical entertainment after the feast in the evening. Guillaume, who was well-known at the castle, since he had long been Beatrice's musical tutor, introduced his wife Bridget and his children Denise, about thirteen, Jack, six, and Marcelline, the baby, aged five, who protested when a maid wanted to take her tambourine away and put it with the other instruments. Said Louise, "Oh, let her keep it for now, what harm is there? Since there are now a number of children here, might they not prefer to go and play in the gardens for a while, instead of being bored by adult chatter?"

So the du Boise family, a number of the other guests' children, including the two sons of Vincent's old school friend, Jason, and another little girl who nobody really knew, but might have been a grandchild of the housekeeper, Mistress Travis, all trotted off happily, together with Timothy, the latest of a long line of household beagles, who was capering about excitedly in anticipation of chasing games.

In a while, some of the guests started to disperse to their guest-rooms to relax and rest before the evening's festivities. As they left, Clotilda fell in beside Vincent, and clutched his arm, saying, "I have no wish to upset your arrangements, Vincent, but I am rather worried about our shop. Master Samuel and his men have undertaken to watch it for us, but he is elderly, and I don't know how seriously his warehousemen will take this duty. Would it be possible for you to go there before dinner and make a few checks? I know this is asking a lot, but I can't help remembering my experiences years ago in Kasselburg with those awful robbers. Even Fritzi, I know, is a little worried, as easygoing as she might appear!"

Vincent patted her shoulder soothingly, "I am glad you asked me, Clotilda, you know I am always ready to help. I will dream myself there, with one or two of our stalwart staff, and set up a proper watch. Please give me the shop keys – and by all means tell Fritzi about this, you shouldn't feel she has to be protected; after all she is a strong person."

He left her, with another reassuring pat, and headed off down the stairs to the servants' hall. There he found some old friends, a gardener called Dickon, and his mate, a groom by the name of Stanley, who were only too eager to fall in with the chance of a little action, since they were simply waiting about to help with "decorations and flowers and such-like", as Dickon said.

Vincent took them into a storeroom and explained about dream travel; neither had experienced it before, but they had confidence in Vincent, for whom they had great respect. He started the humming, and soon the three were high above the countryside, heading for Hastings. They soon caught sight of the sea, and Vincent set them down in front of Samuel's warehouse, seeing that the area was deserted. Dickon and Stanley, of course, were astounded at what they had just experienced, and Vincent allowed them to talk about it for a few minutes, answering a question or two that they had.

The ground floor of the shop was in darkness, but there was lamplight showing at one of the upper windows, and the sounds of laughter and loud talk could be heard in the street below. Some of the loudest voices were male, so Vincent wondered whether Mistress Watson was entertaining visitors, or maybe customers. Walking round to the back of the building, they saw that the builders or shop-fitters had left some timber there, for later collection, no doubt. And there was a ladder, too, so Vincent told his companions to quietly lean it up next to one of the lighted windows "Not that they are likely to hear anything, against the way they are talking now!"

Climbing up the ladder, Vincent was able to peer into the upper room, while keeping in shadow himself. What he saw was somewhat surprising – two women, one old, one young – who he assumed were Mistress Watson and the shop assistant, were sitting with two men, of a coarse and untidy, even dirty, appearance. The four were drinking mugs of what looked like ale, and seemed by their behaviour to have been engaged in this for some time.

Vincent quickly descended the ladder and beckoned his assistants to follow him to the front of the shop, saying "It looks very much to me that Mistress Watson, who is supposed to have responsibility for the shop, has already, after only a day or two, started to behave very badly. It is my opinion that either the two men I saw are complicit with Mistress Watson, or they have duped her. In either case, I have a strong suspicion that they intend to rob the shop, which is stocked with many valuable items; we must prevent this, of course!"

Dickon replied, with a light in his eyes that Vincent thought betokened a desire to engage immediately in conflict, said "Let us go round the back and pick out some stout pieces of timber to use as cudgels! I reckon we could rush them and overcome them very easily. You say there are only two men, and they are likely to be groggy with ale, anyway!"

Chapter 4

As Vincent was about to remonstrate with his eager helpers, to persuade them to take a more prudent course of action, they were accosted by two men in military dress, one with a lantern and the other carrying a staff, who ran up to them from the street.

"Hold there and explain yourselves to the constable!" said the one with the lantern, "Who are you, to be skulking about at night, when all decent folk are safely in their houses? We were called here by a young lad from Samuel's warehouse who espied you on a ladder, trying to climb in through a window."

"I am but an honest citizen doing the work of a constable or watchman!" said Vincent, knowing that his gift of veracity would ensure that these officials would believe him immediately "I and my companions came here to keep an eye on this shop, which is owned by friends of mine, and we have discovered that there is a group of doubtful-looking persons inside, who I believe are planning to rob it!"

"If that be so," replied the constable "we should enter the shop without delay and confront them! Let us break down the door!"

"That sort of violence will not be necessary!" said Vincent, "Look, I have the keys to the shop; let us go in quietly and take these rogues by surprise, if rogues they be! If I'm any judge, they will be befuddled with strong liquors; I could see through the window that they have been drinking. There are but two men in the upper room, in the company of the two women who work in the shop. I suggest that you two officers confront the men, and I will come with you. Dickon and Stanley – find yourselves cudgels from the timber behind the shop and wait each side of the front door to catch these miscreants if they make a dash for it!"

Vincent carefully and quietly unlocked the two locks on the shop front door and stood aside to let the constables, who had each drawn a sword, go in first. Following them, he indicated the stairs, and the three of them mounted, trying not to make a noise. In any case, they could hear that the revelers were still laughing and talking at the top of their voices, and would hardly have heard a stampede of horses.

At the head of the stairs there was only one door visible, so the constables thrust it open and strode in, swords raised. Vincent followed and beheld a scene of carousal. The younger of the two women had by this time been persuaded to sit on the lap of one of the villains, and appeared not to be making any objection to his attentions. The other, Mistress Watson, was sitting back, waving her beer mug and laughing.

When they all espied the constables, they immediately fell silent. The younger woman leapt to her feet, pushing aside the hands of her erstwhile companion, and was the first to gain her voice.

"What is all this?" she cried, "Who do you think you are, breaking into a private party?"

The constable, who seemed to be amused by the proceedings, answered her. "I'll tell you who we are, madam, we are the officers of the law, and we are here to ask you your business and not to answer your questions. Who are you, what are your names, and why are you gathered here?"

Vincent touched the constable's sleeve, and quietly told about his gift of commanding the truth. That officer, surprised at what he had been told, motioned Vincent forward.

Looking the older of the two ruffians in the eyes, Vincent asked him his name and business. To the amazement of the man, and of the others, he answered, without hesitation, "I am Lemuel Hardgraves, of Hastings town, and I am here to rob this shop of whatever valuables I can put my hands on! This here is Billy Billings, from Hastings, too, and he is here to help me and share in the loot!" Vincent could see that the other one was getting very angry at this, so turned his gaze on him and asked, "Well, does he speak truthfully?" To this, the man perforce had to answer "Yes!" and became very subdued.

Without further ado, the constables forced the two men, at sword-point, to allow their wrists to be cuffed behind their backs. The constable then said, "Be thankful that we have grabbed you before you managed to steal anything; you must know that being caught with stolen goods is a hanging offence! The magistrate will likely let you off lightly – in a year or five, with any luck, you will be out of jail again!"

"Now, sir," he said to Vincent, "perhaps you can now ask these two respectable ladies who they are and what they are about!"

By this time both women had got over their indignation, and in fact were weeping in fright. Mistress Watson told her name, and to her intense discomfort had to admit that she knew the men by reputation and had deliberately invited them in, in the full knowledge of their intentions, hoping to share in the proceeds. She further explained that the plan was for she and the shop assistant, who, it turned out, was an old friend of hers, Patience Cummings, to be discovered bound up in the shop, after the robbers had escaped with their loot. Then everyone, including Lady Friederike and Frau Gunther, would have sympathized with them as victims.

After marveling at Vincent's performance, and stating that he wished he had such powers, the constable thanked Vincent very much, and said he would station one of his men at the shop until better arrangements could be made for its security. With that, the four miscreants were marched away, to be locked up in the watch-house until the magistrate would be prepared to try them.

Vincent, Dickon and Stanley made sure that the shop was locked up as securely as possible, and then waited for the watchman to arrive, which he did in less than half an hour.

"Now, we had better get back!" said Vincent, and he started the humming and took his companions back to the castle, where they found that the whole escapade had taken less than two hours, and that the guests had not yet been called to the dining hall.

Vincent took his helpers to the kitchen and cordially thanked them for their support, asking Mistress Travis to make sure they had something special to eat and drink. Then he went up to join the others, most of whom he found in the large sitting room.

Clotilda and Fritzi were, of course, intensely interested to hear his account, were appalled at what might have happened, and vowed that they would take a great deal more trouble when they next engaged any staff!

Lady Louise suggested that maybe they should appoint a male manager next time, and that perhaps they could enquire of Master Samuel whether he knew of anyone suitable. Having met the constables, Vincent further suggested that it might not be a bad idea to ask them to check the candidates as well!

Chapter 5

At the appointed time, a footman traversed the corridors of the castle with a gong, calling everyone to table in the great dining hall. Most guests were settled in their places and they all stood when Pemberton, the majordomo, struck his staff thrice on the floor and announced, "Their Majesties King Arnold and Queen Tabitha!"

The King and Queen entered and took their places at the head of the table, one each side of Louise and Beatrice. After everyone had applauded, and this had been acknowledged by the royal couple, everyone took their seats. Lady Louise then stood to give her welcoming speech.

"Your Majesties, Lords, Ladies and gentlemen – and children, of course – we have all gathered here this evening to honour my beloved daughter, the Lady Beatrice, on the occasion of her twenty-fifth birthday. In our dynasty, that of the de Gonvilles, it is the custom that all the rights of succession and ownership of property are bestowed on a female heir at that age (whereas, I must acknowledge with some small disapproval, a male heir need only wait until he be one-and-twenty). I should make it clear that these rights are distinct from those of the Musgrave Barony and from the ownership of the Woodhampton estates, which have already passed to Brendan."

"Congratulations, my dearest! Let us all make a toast to Beatrice's continuing life and career!"

After the toast, and another to her in response, called for by Vincent, Louise stood once more and continued. "Beatrice has already received her first birthday present, the magnificent jewel given by Konstanze, Ruprecht and Euphemia; and now I will give her the second. Here, my dear, are the title deeds of Bramwell Hall, which I received from the old King and Queen in recognition of a service I gladly rendered them at the time of the treacherous plot! The Hall is currently occupied by some noble tenants, but henceforth it is at your disposal, to do with whatever you wish!" She handed Beatrice a sheaf of parchments, and the two embraced warmly.

There were calls of "Speech, speech!" from the body of the hall, and Beatrice took to her feet.

"I thank you from the bottom of my heart, dear Mama, and I must give my thanks once again to Konstanze, Ruprecht and Euphemia. I am extremely gratified also, by the fact that so many of you have thought it worthwhile to attend these celebrations; such circles of friends and relatives are precious gifts in and of themselves. I must also reveal a magnificent gift from my beloved comrade of many years, Vincent Crabbe, who has often preferred to keep in my shadow; some of you may have noticed, in the corner of this hall, a large object swathed in sheets. Perhaps I can persuade Vincent now to unveil his birthday gift to me – which, I admit, I have already seen and marvelled over – dear Vincent, will you?"

As everyone swivelled round in their seats to watch, Vincent stepped over and whisked off the covering, to disclose a magnificent double manual harpsichord, with shining inlaid brass embellishments and a lid decorated with a pastoral scene, featuring as its centerpiece a beautifully rendered beehive and bees.

Vincent announced "This was built for Beatrice by our mutual friend Master Franz-Johann Steiglitz, of Kasselburg in Hesse. As some may know, Beatrice has been an adept performer on the clavichord over many years, under the tutelage of Guillaume du Boise, and now she can extend her skills, with his guidance, into more sumptuous realms of keyboard music. Beatrice, are you ready to entertain us with a sample?"

"Well," said Beatrice, "I have had but three or four hours of practice on this instrument – I was aware that I might receive this call – but I am willing to expose my shortcomings, if you are prepared to forgive them! However, I will not delay the feasting now, I promise to give a recital after we have all eaten our fill!"

Then Fritzi and Clotilda rose, saying, "If we could delay proceedings just a moment more, we also have a gift for Beatrice!" At their signal, two maids who had been waiting at the side of the hall came forward bearing a large tray between them. It was covered with a linen cloth, and when Beatrice lifted that she found that it had concealed an extensive array of wine-glasses of various sizes as well as two decanters, all engraved with the de Gonville coat of arms. She went to her two friends in turn, embracing them and kissing them on both cheeks, her own wet with tears.

A procession of servants now entered the hall, bearing platters and trenchers with a wonderful variety of dishes, and the assembly were soon engaged in eating, drinking and chatting to their neighbours, while the du Boise children entertained them with a succession of airs and dance tunes, played on flute, lute and tambourine. After half an hour or so, the children bowed to the applause of the guests, and happily ran off to join friends and have their own meals in the small dining room. Du Boise and his wife explained that they would return after dinner, when the dancing and other entertainments would begin.

In between courses, the guests wandered about, renewing acquaintances with old friends and making new ones. Lady Letitia, a cousin of Queen Tabitha, had travelled all the way from Lincolnshire with her new husband, Lord Morgan, and so spent much time introducing him around and catching up with the stories told by her many friends who were visiting from the court at Winchester. The Queen's sister, Lady Margarethe of Bornholm, had declined the invitation, since she was now domiciled in York, and considered that this demanded too long a journey for a merely social purpose.

When people had started to play with scraps on their plates, and the buzz of conversation had settled to a low level, Beatrice announced that she was now ready to embarrass herself by essaying to play the harpsichord, which brought a chorus of encouraging refutation from the assembly. She sat down at the keyboard, and for the next half an hour played a selection of pieces, starting with straightforward items, but culminating in a lively dance tune, full of trills and other ornaments. Guillaume du Boise could be observed to have an expression of indulgent approval on his countenance, and, of course, the recital brought a chorus of approbation, some of the younger guests even stamping their feet!

Beatrice returned to her place with an expression of relief, and was hugged by her Mama as she resumed her seat.

Next came a surprise item; Euphemia and her new sister-in-law Konstanze came forward and regaled the audience with several duets, sung without accompaniment, mostly in German, but finishing with a traditional English ballad which brought enthusiastic applause, some of the younger women even joining in with the refrain! After that, dancing and card playing broke out generally, and looked set to continue all night!

Chapter 6

The next day, it was towards noon before most of the guests bestirred themselves. Some, especially the young ones, felt peckish and found their way to the small dining room, where there was a range of hot and cold foods and drinks laid out; others sought fresh air and sunshine and wandered into the gardens and terraces. Beatrice went to her mother's apartment and found her being dressed by her maid.

"What are your feelings about the party?" asked Louise, "Were you happy at what transpired? I was watching the King and Queen particularly, and if their reactions are any guide, the evening was a great success!"

"Oh yes, Mama, I also felt happy and gratified, but as a good hostess, I have been wondering what activities we could offer our guests from now onward – some of them will be staying in Woodhampton for up to a week, of course. I did think of asking Fritzi to take some people riding to explore our beautiful local countryside; we have a sufficiency of palfreys in our stables to mount a half-dozen or so. And there are others who would like to go boating, I would conjecture – apart from the river we could take them to the lake on the Chelsfield estate, where there are several skiffs and punts always kept in the boatshed."

"Those are some good ideas," replied Louise, "but we should not forget those guests, especially the older ones, who might prefer less energetic diversions and would want to stay indoors; I warrant that there will be many keen card players among both the ladies and the gentlemen. I saw some enthusiasm developing in that direction late last night!"

"And, besides," added Beatrice, "two ladies have enquired of me already whether they might be allowed to play my harpsichord while they are here; one of them, it was Lady Letitia Morgan, if I remember rightly, told me she had brought music with her for voice, lute and keyboard, and was going to ask the little du Boise girl, Denise, to join her and one or two of her friends. The hall will soon be filled with mellifluous strains – I hope they will be mellifluous, anyway!"

"That reminds me," said Louise, "it is some time since you, Vincent, the twins, and our other little friends who had been able to transform into other creatures, lost this power because of their inevitable maturity. I have been meaning to sound out some parents to see whether they would be willing for their children to be vouchsafed such a gift. I thought, particularly, of Jack and Marcelline du Boise – I imagine their elder sister, Denise, who is thirteen, I believe, has already missed the opportunity. I'll speak to Guillaume and Bridget today – are there any others whose families we know well enough for me to approach?"

At that moment, there was a knock on the door and Brendan put his head in, saying, "If you are not too busy, Mama?" When Louise said that she and Beatrice were a little busy, but could be interrupted, Brendan came fully into the room, bringing with him, hand-in-hand, a shy young woman, who Louise had seen at dinner the night before, but who had not been introduced.

"May I present Lady Florence Chippenham, eldest daughter of the Duke and Duchess of Dorset! Florence, please to meet my Mama, Lady Louise de Gonville, and my sister, Lady Beatrice. We have an announcement to make – I have asked for Florence's hand in marriage, and she has graciously accepted! She is not yet of age, so she will seek her parents' permission later today – they are both here in the castle. Perhaps, if they agree, we can make a formal announcement to all present at dinner this evening."

Louise exclaimed with pleasure, "This is indeed good news, Brendan!" and warmly embraced the young woman; this greeting was immediately repeated by Beatrice, who kissed her and hugged her tightly. Then said Louise, "Please leave us, Brendan and Beatrice, I need to converse long and searchingly with my future daughter-in-law and discover her life and likings!"

As they left the room, Brendan and Beatrice saw their mother draw Florence to sit beside her on a couch, kissing her cheek once again.

As they descended the staircase, Beatrice took her brother by the hand, saying, "This is a most unexpected but welcome event, Brendan – I took you for a confirmed bachelor! How long is it that you and Florence have known one another?"

"Since last evening!" was his surprising reply, "I danced a few measures of the estampie as her partner and that was sufficient! And I think that she has taken to me as quickly – I am so happy! My only concern is whether her parents will be as enthusiastic –

what I dread is that they will impose upon us a long engagement period."

As they entered the small dining room, Beatrice saw that Vincent was just leaving, going apparently in the direction of the gardens. She gave Brendan a quick peck on the cheek, and ran after Vincent, caught him up and seized his arm.

"You'll never guess!" she exclaimed, "It appears as though my foolish brother is growing up at last – no, I must not be too unfair, he has really been a lot quieter lately! Anyway, he says he is engaged to be married – how exciting!"

"Yes, I thought I saw Brendan and a young lady in intimate conversation last night – I do hope he is serious, it would be a great pity if such a quiet, nice-looking, young woman were to be disappointed. Maybe I will get a chance to catechise him on the subject before it is too late! – Or would this be too prudent and interfering? After all it is the lady's parents who must make such a judgment."

Lady Louise talked with Florence for some time, asking her about her feelings, of course, and finally came to the conclusion that the young woman was entering into this enterprise with her eyes open and in a sincere spirit. She gave Florence her blessing and then asked for Brendan to be found; she had a similar long conversation with him, in the knowledge that he was obliged to speak truthfully to her, and again finished with a sense of satisfaction about his intentions.

Later that day, at a family conference between Lady Louise and Florence's parents, the Duke and Duchess, a lengthy discussion focused on whether or not the engagement would be allowed to go ahead. An agreement was reached on this, but as Brendan had feared, a period of six months would be stipulated before the marriage could take place, and as the ultimate test, the couple would be required to dwell together, in Woodhampton Castle, but closely chaperoned by Lady Hermione Bagshott, the older sister of the Duchess, for all that time.

And Florence admitted, in some relief, that if a chaperone were really needed, she would as soon she be Aunt Hermione as anyone else.

And, at dinner that evening, the official announcement was made by Henry, the Duke of Dorset, before King Arnold and Queen Tabitha and all the guests assembled, to much toasting.

Chapter 7

On the next day, as Beatrice had hoped, four or five guests rode out, with Fritzi as their guide, to explore the countryside round Woodhampton, Beatrice not losing the chance to point out the famous dene-hole in the woods where, as she related, Vincent and she had first met, so many years ago.

And a carriage-load of energetic young guests were taken to Chelsfield Hall, where Vincent initiated them into the skills of rowing a skiff or poling a punt in the large but shallow ornamental lake in the grounds.

All returned to Woodhampton with famous appetites for luncheon!

After luncheon, Lady Louise had invited a select group to her apartment, and Beatrice and Vincent joined her in welcoming them. As well as Queen Tabitha and the new Landgravine, Countess Konstanze, there were Fritzi and Clotilda and several little children – Jack and Marcelline du Boise, Hannah Travis, the house-keeper's granddaughter and her friend Winnie, an orphan who had been taken in by Mistress Travis.

They were all sat down on couches around Louise's sitting room, looking somewhat uncertain of the reason for their presence, given the seemingly strange mixture of persons present, but Louise soon started to explain.

"Your Majesty, Konstanze, Friederike and Clotilda and dear children, most of you are aware that I, my daughter Beatrice and Master Vincent Crabbe, are all possessed of certain arcane powers – you have seen some of them in action. We have already bestowed these precious gifts on a few trusted friends and family, including Princess Euphemia and the Landgrave Ruprecht of Hesse. And now, we thought it time to vouchsafe these arcane powers, in their several combinations, to some further deserving souls. I will start with the children so that they may not become impatient!"

She stood, Beatrice and Vincent on each side, and said sweetly, "Marcelline, Hannah, Winnie and Jack, please come here to me! Please close your eyes; do not be afeared, this will be very comfortable!"

The four children lined up before her, eyes shut, and, in turn, Louise took each of their faces between her hands for a few moments, whispering in their ears. Then she said, "You may open your eyes now, and I will explain your new gifts!"

"For the nonce, I have bestowed a single power on each of you; when you are older, there will be more! You may not feel any different yet, but from this moment onward each of you can transform yourself into other forms! Now tell me, Marcelline, what is your favourite creature?"

Little Marcelline thought for a moment and then said "Pussy-cat!"

The same question was put to the others, Jack nominating a dog, Hannah a bunny-rabbit, and Winnie, strangely, a goat.

Lady Louise continued, "Now, dear children, I want you all to sit on the couches, close your eyes, and pretend you are turning into your favourite!"

They did so, and, one by one, a cat, a small dog and a rabbit were seen to appear in their places. But Winnie stayed Winnie!

As the first three creatures opened their eyes and looked about them, Louise went and knelt in front of Winnie, who still had her eyes firmly shut. She took her hands, saying, "Tell me Winnie, what are you thinking?" "Oh, my lady," replied the little girl, "I thought it improper for a goat to be seen in your nice clean sitting-room!" Louise smiled and kissed her, "Believe me, dear child, there have been stranger sights than that in this room! Do not worry, it is perfectly fine for you to become a goat! Please go ahead now."

And, sure enough, a small white goat was seen to take shape!

Lady Louise clapped her hands and said, "Now children, close your eyes again and imagine you are regaining your true shape! Do not be disappointed, you will have this power for a long time, to be used whenever you wish, but I would like to tell you some more about it now."

The adults, who had been fascinated by the proceedings, waited patiently while Louise explained that the gift was precious, not to be used idly, for sport, or to impress friends, and that they would find it could not be used for evil, nor to give harm. And then, Louise kissed each child and sent it away to carry on with its day's activities.

Then Louise turned to the adults, saying, "Not one of you may receive the gift of transformation you have just witnessed; it is only capable of being bestowed on young children before they start to take on the attributes of maturity. In time, each of those children will lose that gift, but, by that time, I will have given them others that will console them in their loss. Now, let us turn to you, my friends!"

"The first gift is that of tongues, the ability to understand and to speak in any language of the world. Some of you will find this immensely valuable, some may never have occasion to use it. The next gift I regard as the most precious of all, and is one that has been of great benefit to me and my circle over the years; it is the gift of veracity. When one who has this gift looks in a person's eyes, that person is compelled to speak nothing but the truth. And, conversely, the one with the gift is compelled likewise to speak truly – this is the price of the gift – but will be believed implicitly by any listener. I, of course, have this gift, so do you believe me?" Her audience smiled and nodded, turning to each other for verification.

Louise continued, "There is one further gift, but we shall leave that for another day; it is the gift of dream travel. You, Konstanze, already know what this entails, since Euphemia and Ruprecht brought you hither with its aid. But I think that we have encountered enough new things today. Let us proceed. Please join your hands, all four."

Louise went to each of them in turn, again taking their faces between her hands and whispering into each ear. Then she asked them to sit down on the couches. "I, Beatrice and Vincent will come to you one by one and make sure that the gift of tongues has taken hold in each of you. Some of you are already fluent in several languages, so we will pick something arcane for this test. Starting with you, your Majesty, are you conversant with Arabic? No? Well you are now, let us see!" There followed a long conversation in that tongue, with Queen Tabitha's expression becoming more and more delighted.

The next half hour was taken up in similar ways, and each of those who had received the gifts expressed their gratitude. Clotilda, in particular, saying, "Now Fritzi and I shall be able to find an honest manager without any doubt whatsoever!"

Konstanze, in her quiet way, simply smiled to herself.

Chapter 8

Some of the guests, including the King and Queen, were not able to stay very much longer, so over the remainder of that day, and on into the next morning, they came to thank their hosts one by one and to go the rounds of the castle to say goodbye to the other guests, some promising to maintain contact with those they had met at Woodhampton for the first time.

Among those who came to bid farewell to Louise and Beatrice first thing the next day were the Duke and Duchess of Dorset, who also wished to introduce Lady Hermione Bagshott to them so that they could all discuss the arrangements that would need to be made so that she could fulfill her role as chaperone for the young betrothed couple.

Louise took the three into her sitting room, sat them down and rang for refreshments; she asked the maid who came in response to her ring to make sure also that Lord Brendan and Lady Florence were informed that Lady Louise and the Duke and Duchess desired their company. While they waited, the proud parents told Louise of their daughter, of her accomplishments and of her character, "She appears exceedingly quiet, I must admit," said her father, "but withal she has some spirit, once it is aroused! But dear Hermione will not have any difficulty in maintaining control, I am sure! But what of Brendan, Louise?"

"Well, my son has certainly had his foolish moments when he was younger!" replied Louise, "But, particularly since his accession to the title, he seems to have become quite sensible and straightforward, I am glad to say!"

The maid returned with a companion, bearing trays of cakes and drinks, set them down and then curtseyed to Lady Louise, saying, "I told Mr Pemberton of your request, my lady, and he said he would see to it immediately. But that was hardly ten minutes since." The two maids bobbed again and left the room.

Louise and her guests carried on discussing arrangements further, as they nibbled and sipped the refreshments, but after twenty minutes or so, there was a knock on the door and the majordomo, Pemberton, entered, looking a little flushed.

"I'm sorry, my lady, but I am informed by the stable master that the young couple left in a chaise early this morning, Lord Brendan driving. He was not informed where they were going, nor when they would return, and he did not feel he should ask."

The Duke was rather peeved at this, "You would think that they would have told someone of their plans! Now, I suppose, we shall have simply to cool our heels until they deign to return!"

The Duchess, seeing that Louise was rather distressed at all this, went to her and consoled her, putting her arm round her shoulders, while Lady Hermione pursed her lips and tut-tutted in exasperation, exclaiming, "Do they not realize what is meant by being chaperoned? They could be getting up to all sorts of high jinks! Wait till they return and I will give both of them a piece of my mind!"

Mr Pemberton withdrew, saying that he would make further enquiries, but returned not five minutes later, holding a letter. "The chambermaid brought me this a moment ago, saying it had been left on Lord Brendan's desk in his living room. It is addressed to Lady Louise."

Louise took it from him, her hand trembling, either with anger or anxiety, opened it, started to read, and then read it aloud.

" 'Dear Mama,' " it starts, she said, " 'Florence and I have been talking, and we have decided that it will be impossible for us to wait as long as six months before being wed. Consequently, we are going to drive to a place where we are not known, find a country parson, take lodgings in his village and have him read the banns. After three readings, we shall be married.' "

"He then goes on to make some sanctimonious apologies for the trouble they are causing us! The wretch – I blame him for leading Florence astray!" And Louise started to weep.

"Now, now, my dear Louise!" interjected the Duke, "Let us not start attributing blame, but think how we might forestall this senseless act! Fortunately enough the necessity for reading the banns has given us a space to think and act. How far can a chaise drive in a day? Will Brendan spare the horse (I am assuming it was a one-horse chaise), or will he ask much of the poor beast? Let us send for the stable master and see what he thinks; he would know the horse and the carriage."

Louise rang for her maid again and asked for the stable master to be summoned; then she added, "We should also find out whether the watchers on the battlements noticed which road was taken; it may be possible to send one of our newly-gifted children, in the form of a bird, to follow the road and see whether the chaise can be tracked down. I am a little reluctant to do this, since they are all rather young and inexperienced; I would have preferred to send someone a little older."

"Well, Mama," put in Beatrice, "It may not be too late to endow another child with the gift of transformation; who can we think of who is old enough, but not too old?"

"Of course!" said Louise, clapping her hands, "There must be a twelve or thirteen-year old around – preferably a boy, since they mature later and may be more enterprising! Let us think deeply. Beatrice, please go and fetch Vincent, the more heads we can put together, the better."

Beatrice came back with Vincent at the same time that the stable master, Mr Potter, was arriving at the door. They ushered him in, in front of them, and the Duke asked him about the chaise, the horse and how far he thought was a good day's drive.

"Well, I have known Master Brendan – I mean Lord Brendan – since I used to let him sit on the box next to me as I drove the carriage between here and Winchester. He may be a little wild, but I have never known him to be anything but considerate to a horse. That chaise is very light, and I would say that it could keep a good speed all day. I would guess that it might take them, shall we say, ninety miles, between seven o'clock when they left, and this evening, when they would be wanting to find a place for the night."

At these words, the Duchess let out a low moan, saying, "I fear that they might take only one room! Oh, please let that not be the case!" Louise put her hand on her arm and patted it, saying "Let us not jump to too many conclusions; they showed no signs of undue familiarity around the castle, so far!"

The stable master continued, "I am told they set off along the road we used to take to Winchester, but of course there would be nothing to prevent them turning off anywhere."

At this point, Vincent spoke, saying, "I have thought of a likely child to send after them as a bird! Why not Mr Pemberton's son, Wilfred? I think he is twelve years old, and a steady lad."

Chapter 9

Before very long, Wilfred Pemberton had been found playing catch with a couple of friends in the garden and brought to Louise's sitting room. He looked a little apprehensive, so Louise quickly put him at his ease, and Vincent, who had known him for a year or two, explained that they had an important task for him, which would save Lord Brendan considerable trouble later on. This gave the lad enough confidence to enquire what it might entail, so Louise explained.

"Do you know, Wilfred, that it is possible for some young lasses and lads to change their shapes, and take on the form and abilities of any creature?"

"I have heard of this, my lady; they say that Lady Beatrice was able to do this when she was younger, but I know not whether this be a fable or no."

Louise smiled, and took his hands, "It is no fable, my child, and I can give you that power if you are willing; we need someone to seek out Lord Brendan and his fiancée, for they have foolishly taken their leave of their families and the rest of us without due thought!"

"I will accept this mission willingly, my lady, if you say that it is proper!"

Lady Louise took his face between her hands, asked him to close his eyes, and whispered softly "I hereby endow you, Wilfred, with the gift of transformation, to be used for good and not for idle sport nor to do harm. Now, if you were to choose the form of a bird capable of travelling fast and long, which would it be?"

Wilfred thought for a moment and then said, "Why, my lady, a swallow or swift might be a good choice!"

Louise smiled and nodded, "So, sit on the couch, close your eyes and imagine yourself becoming a swallow! You will be able to understand human speech, but you will have to wait until you regain your own shape before you can tell us how it is, meanwhile, we will still be able to give you your instructions!"

The lad hesitated a moment, and then those watching saw him diminish in size and take on the form of a swallow. Vincent took him up, and let him perch on his fist.

Then, between them, Louise, Beatrice and Vincent explained what had happened and what they wanted Wilfred to do.

"Do you know the one-horse chaise that is kept in our stables, what it looks like?" said Vincent. The swallow nodded its little head.

"We are told that Lord Brendan and Lady Florence were last seen departing on the road that leads to Winchester, so what you should do first is fly in that direction. Lord Brendan has informed his Mama that they are looking for a parish where they are not known, so this must mean that he would have wanted to put some miles behind them. Try flying along the main road, but at a height that will give you a wide view. The weather is clear today, so you should be able to see a fair distance."

Beatrice added, "You must not get yourself lost, of course, so mark well how you travel! If you fly fast, you can travel in one hour as far as the chaise will go in four or five, I should think. But, if you have not found them before night begins to fall, just come back and tell us, we will not think less of thee! If you have any questions of us now, just change back to Wilfred and ask!"

And then Louise made it clear that he was not to engage in conversation with the pair, but merely to take note of where they were heading, or where they had decided to stay. And she gave him a final piece of advice "Remember that you are not bound to stay a swallow – if it seems necessary, change back to yourself or to another creature – I believe that you are a lad with enough wit to make wise decisions! Now go, our blessings go with you!"

The little bird took wing and flew out through the open window as confidently as though he was born to be a bird.

Lady Louise drew herself up, sighed and said, "All we can do now is wait and hope! Let us go and inform the Duke and Duchess – and it must be almost luncheon time, by now!"

They went to the small dining room, where they enjoyed luncheon in the company of Lady Hermione and the Duke and Duchess. The only subject of conversation, of course was the hunt for Brendan and Florence; Louise tried to placate the others, saying that even if Wilfred was unsuccessful on this occasion, there would be plenty of time remaining, saying "We have still two days before the banns can be read this Sunday, and after that there will need to be a fortnight's wait before a wedding can be permitted. And all this is supposing the foolish pair is able to persuade this parish priest to marry them, and there is no certainty that he will agree to such a proposition that is made by strangers."

Elfrida, the Duchess, had further worries "The wedding is our main concern, certainly, but what of their behaviour before then? They are young, and in love, so will they be able to restrain themselves for two weeks? Florence is a quiet girl and has always been a model of decorum, but the circumstances are different now and I know not how well Lord Brendan might be able to hold his feelings in check, when they are thrown together in some quiet inn for a few days."

While they were thus discussing, young Wilfred entered the room, peering around to find them, and then almost running to them in excitement, exclaiming "I have found the chaise, hard by a church, in a village not many miles from here!"

He was sat down next to the anxious parents, and was given a cool drink and calmed down by Lady Louise, who said, "Slowly, slowly, my boy, get back your breath and tell us all about it – did you see Lord Brendan and Lady Florence?"

"No, my lady, not immediately! You had told me not to talk to the couple themselves, but I judged that I was allowed to speak to others, as long as I was discreet. So I alighted next the chaise and regained my human form. There was a lad there, who told me he had been given a penny to hold the horse's head while the lady and gentleman went to the church. So I went there myself, and when I saw that I was not overlooked, I changed myself into a little mouse, thinking that I would not be easily noticed like that. I stole through the main door of the church and found the vestry, in which I could hear some people in conversation with a young priest. The door was open, so I slipped in and hid under the desk. I would not eavesdrop like that normally, of course, but this was different."

The listeners were all agog at this account, and urged him to continue. "I soon heard Lord Brendan mention his name, and so I listened intently. The next to speak was the priest, but what he said seemed to dismay the young couple!"

Chapter 10

Wilfred paused at this point in his account and his listeners leant closer, "The priest proceeded to explain that he could have done what he was asked, but for the fact that Brendan and Florence were not his parishioners. He said that he would have to seek leave from his bishop to marry folk from elsewhere, or else would need letters from their own parish priests. From where I was, under the desk, I could hear Brendan give a snort of disbelief, and Florence start to weep. Then Brendan asked a question 'Father, I understand what you say. Would it make any difference were I to bolster my credentials by making a large donation to your church? I noticed that the spire is in urgent need of repair, and you have but two rows of pews in a space that would take ten at least.' "

Lady Louise could not contain herself, "How Brendan betrays himself – he thinks that money is the answer to every problem! I could box his ears, as old as he is! But go on, Wilfred, what was the priest's answer?"

"The priest simply laughed, and said that Brendan was misguided, but that there might be a way, after all, 'If you both were to reside in this village for a week, you would become members of my parish – this would delay the reading of the banns for only a few days! What do you say?' to which Brendan replied 'We will do it – but where shall we stay? Is there an inn, we did not see one in the village as we drove here?' The priest said that he was right, but that it might be possible for them to be taken in as boarders by one or other of the cottagers. At that point, I could hear and see them all rising to their feet, so I quickly scurried out of the vestry, made my way out of the church, transformed to a swallow once more and flew swiftly back here to report to you."

Louise embraced him, while the others congratulated him on his achievement. Said Duke Henry, "Now we have even more time to act. Tell us, Wilfred, were you able to discover the name of the village and of the church?"

"Yes, my lord, I asked the lad who was minding the horse. The village is called Dunton Green, and the church is Saint Anthony's. I did not stay long enough to find out whether the couple managed to settle on a place to stay. They will also have to find stabling and feed for their horse, I suppose."

The Duchess was still anxious about the accommodation arrangements, remarking, "I do hope they are staying chaste until the wedding! If they do not, the wedding ceremony itself becomes somewhat of a superfluity, in my view!"

"Besides," added Lady Hermione, "I cannot fulfil my duties as a chaperone under these circumstances! I blame myself for taking my eyes off them so that they were able to slip away like this!"

"Now, now, Hermione," replied the Duchess, "you did everything that could be expected of you, short of chaining yourself to them, so do not fret on that score!"

Lady Louise decided to become practical, "Instead of worrying, let us see what we can do. First, now we know their whereabouts (or at least, where they were an hour since), we can intercept them as they search for lodgings. Let Beatrice and I dream Elfrida and ourselves to that village straight away, while Henry and Vincent – and Hermione, too, since she is so concerned – drive there in a carriage, taking Wilfred as their guide. And, in due time, we shall all meet at St. Anthony's church. Wilfred – how far is it, how long did it take you to fly home? Less than an hour, wasn't it? In such a case it should be possible to drive there in four hours at the most. Let us all go, with no further delay!"

As Louise and her companions approached the village – Wilfred's instructions had been easy to follow – they could see the chaise in front of a cottage, with the horse tethered and grazing on a nearby green. They alighted at the side of the cottage and gave Elfrida a few minutes to gather herself after an experience so strange to her. Then they went to the front door and knocked. They heard movement inside, and a woman, wiping flour from her hands, opened the door and gazed enquiringly at them without speaking.

"Good day to you, Mistress," said Louise, "we are sorry if we interrupt you in your baking, but we are looking for some young relatives of ours. We noticed their chaise outside and surmised they might be within."

"Well, my lady," said the woman, trying to curtsey a little, but finding it difficult because of her girth, "the young lady and her husband were here a while ago, but they have gone looking for somewhere to stay – I could not take them as lodgers, for I have no suitable room."

"Do you know where they went?"

"I said they could try Mistress Harper, for she has just married off her daughter and has a room to spare. Her cottage is yonder, the one with the creepers climbing up the trellis by the front door. I know not whether they are still there, but that is where they went to from here."

Thanking the woman, the ladies turned and set out across the green to the cottage that had been pointed out. As they passed the grazing horse, he raised his head and regarded them.

As they walked, Elfrida continued her fretting, "Did you hear the woman say 'her husband'? I'll warrant they are passing themselves off as married already – let us make haste!"

At the front door of the cottage, Louise was just about to knock, when the door opened and who should come out but Brendan, hand-in-hand with Florence!

He recoiled from his mother in surprise, and Florence burst into floods of tears and clung to him. There followed a somewhat animated conversation.

A half-hour later found them all seated in the church, for want of anywhere else to go. Hearing their voices, still high-pitched and excited, the young priest emerged from his vestry and enquired what was afoot. He recognized Brendan and Florence immediately, of course, and the others explained who they each were, and what their business.

He nodded and smiled, in a way that revealed that he had grasped the situation straight away, asked if he might speak privately to the young couple, and led them into the vestry, closing the door firmly behind them. The door remained closed for twenty minutes, during which time the Duchess clung to Louise, sobbing with relief on her shoulder. Louise did no more than pat her consolingly, saying, "There, there!" and the like.

When the priest emerged, Florence went to her mother and embraced her, while Brendan, too, approached his own mother, knelt in front of her and begged her forgiveness, saying, "We have now been convinced that a six-month engagement is not such a big impediment to our happiness after all!"

Chapter 11

With the safe return and settling down of Brendan and Florence, life at Woodhampton castle once again began to return to normality – rather too quickly, it seemed to some.

Lady Louise was, therefore, very pleased when the majordomo came to her one afternoon to announce, "My lady, the master builder, Gerald Hutchinson, is here to report to you about the works on the accommodation for Lord Brendan and Lady Florence. Shall I show him in?"

"By all means, Mr Pemberton, I hope he has good news for me! Would you please go to tell Lady Hermione, too, and ask her if she would like to join us – she will be very interested, I am sure."

The builder came in, rather dusty and gripping his cap. "Good day to you, my lady, I'm glad to say that we're almost done, here. The painters will have finished the doors in an hour or so, they tell me. As we arranged when we were talking with you and Lady Hermione before, we've knocked out a wall between the old Lord's apartments (rest his soul) and one of the guest suites, changed the doors around and now we've got three bedrooms and suites, the middle one for Lady Hermione, with the others leading off, then a big shared sitting room, and studies for Lord Brendan and for Lady Florence; the staff have already moved her clavichord into that one. Soon as the rest of the furniture has been moved in, the young persons and Lady Hermione can settle in properly. There's a bit of repairing to be done on the paneling, here and there, and some plasterwork on one of the ceilings still needs fixing, but those artisans can do their work without disturbing anyone much."

"Why, thank you Mr Hutchinson, it sounds as though you have done splendidly!" said Louise, "Will you show me round now? I'll take the occupants through the apartments myself, this evening, they are all out riding with Lady Beatrice at the moment."

One of the two private studies was meant for Brendan – he was taking over an increasing load of the duties of administering the Woodhampton estates, and the other was for Florence, for her studies and her music – she had gratefully accepted Beatrice's clavichord, which Master Gottfried had refurbished for her, and she was being instructed in its playing by Guillaume du Boise. Hermione was glad that the instrument was rather quiet, so that Florence's practicing would not disturb her, "Besides, her study is not right next to my room and, in any case I rather enjoy some music from time to time – she is becoming more skilful day by day."

Master Arbutius had offered to give Florence some lessons in the English classics and history, since her former education, although of a high standard, had been based on the Germanic traditions beloved of her mother, who was of Bavarian stock. He had other pupils at the castle, too, most of them the children or grandchildren of senior staff members, but as he often said, half seriously, "Beatrice is now more of a scholar than I!"

Satisfied with her inspection of the building work, Lady Louise thanked the builder, saying he should present his accounts to Mr Pemberton without delay. And as soon as Brendan and Florence returned to the castle after their ride, she took them and Lady Hermione around and told them that if they lacked for any extra furniture or decorations they had only to ask. They seemed very happy, and Florence gave Louise a hug and a kiss.

Happy at the eventual outcome with their daughter, the Duke and Duchess of Dorset had taken their leave and driven to their home in the West, and the King and Queen were back in Winchester. So now, as Beatrice declared, rather wistfully, at dinner that night, "It looks as though my birthday celebrations are almost at an end – and Euphemia, Ruprecht and Konstanze will be deserting me too, before long!"

At that, Euphemia came round the table to console her, saying, "Well, dear Beatrice, unless you have pressing duties here in Woodhampton, we were proposing to invite you, and Vincent, too, if he would like, to pay a visit to us in Schloss Kirschbaum, and to stay as long as you would enjoy, so you may consider this as part of your birthday! The weather in Hesse is beautiful at this time of the year, so we might also consider taking a tour or two, to the mountains, perhaps, or to the lakes. You have never seen much more of the countryside than the river and road between Schloss Kirschbaum and Kasselburg, have you?"

Beatrice clapped her hands at this, and smothered Euphemia with kisses. Her thoughts, as usual for her, then raced ahead, "We should go by ship and carriage, instead of dreaming ourselves there – it is a long time since I have had the chance of such a sight-seeing trip!"

Vincent was beaming, too, saying, "I also look forward to this; I have in any case wanted for some time to have a talk and exchange experiences with Wilhelm Steffanhaus, old Konrad's successor as the beekeeper of Schloss Kirschbaum; I have a lot to tell him of the new types of hives and different methods I have been working out. My right-hand man, old Nathaniel's son Ezra, has been learning fast from his father and me, and I have no hesitation in leaving him to look after the hives while I'm away."

"And, Beatrice, I think we ought to take along young Wilfred; what do you say? That lad deserves some reward for the way he helped us with the runaways, and besides, it is always useful, should some unforeseen circumstance arise, to have the company of at least one who can change his shape."

So Potter was informed that the large coach and two drivers would be needed for the next morning, and Mistress Travis was asked to prepare hampers enough for the trip to Hastings and the sea crossing. Beatrice said, "Since the inns in France and Hesse serve such cheap and delicious meals, we will not need to cater for ourselves once we are across the channel. One of us will dream travel to Hastings this evening, to make sure of booking a passage for tomorrow, but Fritzi and Clotilda tell us that they have never had any trouble finding passage for themselves and cargo for the crossing to Boulogne. The bulk of the heavy trade plies from the Kentish ports, as well as London and Harwich, I am told."

There ensued much packing of valises and much discussion of what to put in them, mainly by the ladies. Ruprecht had been sharing clothes with Vincent to some extent while he was in Woodhampton, since the dream travelers had only brought with them a few outfits each, while Euphemia and Konstanze, it must be said, had been freely buying clothes in other towns in England during their stay; as Euphemia had remarked, "What is the point of going home with only the same fashions that we were wearing when we left? How can we impress our friends and relations in Hesse like that?"

Said Beatrice, "Of course! I shall certainly be looking over the latest styles that can be bought in Schloss Kirschbaum and elsewhere while we are away!"

33

Chapter 12

Vincent dreamed himself to Hastings straight after dinner, and went to the Barbary Inn, which he knew was the favourite haunt of many of the seafarers when they were in port. As he opened the front door of the main saloon, he was greeted by a cacophony of sounds – laughing, singing, and quarrelling, as well as a rich mixture of the smells of beer, wine and unwashed sailors. He pushed his way to the bar and asked the barman if he could point out the masters of any ships that might be sailing the next day.

The man, handing him a mug of ale, said, "Why, Sir, if you're looking for a passage, you would do no better than to visit that table over in the far corner – those gentry there are all master mariners, so you'll likely find someone to help you amongst them."

As he made his way over to the corner, Vincent didn't pay much attention to a stout woman who was walking about, collecting used mugs. As he passed by her, she looked at him intently.

At the table, Vincent greeted the men and asked "Captains all, is there any one of you sailing across to France tomorrow, or in a day or two, who would have space aboard for seven or eight passengers, a coach and horses and a quantity of luggage? We are prepared to pay very well for such a service."

A couple of the drinkers laughed, as though he was jesting, but a swarthy man with his long black hair caught up in a pigtail spoke up, "Well, your honour, I can certainly take you and your companions and their luggage, and I have a friend docking tomorrow morning who is accustomed to carrying livestock and heavy freight, such as your coach. If you are prepared to wait in Boulogne for a day or so, he will bring your coach over, together with the driver or someone to tend to the horses, I'm sure – we can speak to him tomorrow when he arrives. Is the rest of your party in Hastings now? My name is Captain Kellogg, Albert, and the friend of whom I speak is Captain Henri Beaumartin – he is a Frenchy, but a decent man withal!"

Vincent shook the man's hand warmly, saying, "My name is Vincent Crabbe. What if we all meet you at the dockside at noon tomorrow; I can be sure that all of my party will be able to arrive by then. What is your ship, and where is she tied up?"

"That sounds admirable, Mr Crabbe, I command the three-master *Belle of Sussex*, and she is moored at the town wharf – anyone at the docks will direct you there. I will not know about Henri's ship until she docks, but we can sort all that out tomorrow – it will be a pleasure to do business with you, sir!"

They shook hands again, and drank a toast to the venture, and Vincent bade farewell to Captain Kellogg and his friends and made his way to the door.

As he left the inn, his eyes took a while to adjust to the darkness of the night; he stood still for a moment, making sure he would not be observed as he started the humming for dream travel, when suddenly he was seized roughly from behind by two tall powerful men who grasped both his arms. Then someone flashed a lantern in his face and a woman's voice said, "You're not so brave when you haven't the constables to back you up, are you, Mr High-and-mighty Vincent!" She then said to the two assailants, "This is the one, right enough; I'll be bound he thought that Mistress Watson would still be rotting in the watch-house – well she ain't, so you see!"

"But poor Lemmy and Bill are thrown in the jail, and will be there for more'n five years, thanks to you. If it weren't for the fact I'm a good liar when I ain't being magicked, I'd be with 'em, too! That magistrate thought that Patience and me might be good for a bit of fun besides, I reckon, but we wouldn't waste our time with old sticks like him, neither of us."

Addressing her confederates, she said, "Don't let him look at you, he's got some wizardry about him. Best not to speak to him at all, or he'll have you saying things you don't want! Drag him over to our old stables, we can put him there until we can think of the best way of squeezing money out of him – he must have plenty! And if he hasn't, so much the worse for him, we'll give him a drubbing he won't forget for a year or two."

Vincent was half-dragged, half-carried to a rambling building facing the inn. The woman unlocked a huge padlock securing an iron bolt, and Vincent was pitched inside, tripping over something and falling heavily on his face, fortunately onto straw covering the floor, which betrayed by its aroma the recent presence of horses.

The three slammed the door, and Vincent could hear that it was being locked again, Mistress Watson calling out, "Have a restful night, sir, we'll bring your breakfast and call in for the room rent in the morning!" She and her companions left, laughing and slapping hands to celebrate a good job done.

As Vincent started his humming, he imagined their reactions when they arrived the next morning – but he would have to make sure that none of his party let their vigilance slip. These people would have several scores to settle!

Back at Woodhampton Castle he related all this to an enthralled audience, warning everyone to be sure to keep together and watch one another's backs. "These villains will be looking for me in particular, of course, but if I am seen in your company they might widen their target. We should arrange our travel so that we are at the docks not too long before noon, so that we can embark with dispatch. Once we are on board Captain Kellogg's vessel, we should be out of danger, because he will have deckhands aplenty. Which drivers are we taking?"

"Well," said Lady Louise, "Potter will go, of course – he is very reliable and resourceful – and I think the other will be that tall young Earnshaw; as well as being an excellent coachman, I believe he used to play the game of football until Mr Pemberton forbade it as too dangerous, when two men from the next village had their limbs broken. He is certainly someone that I would like to have on my side in a battle!"

Beatrice had been thinking seriously, "We should report all this to the constables, too. They already know dear Mistress Watson and they will surely be aware of other dangerous characters who frequent the harbour area of the town. Did you get a glimpse of your assailants, Vincent?"

Vincent could see that Euphemia and Konstanze were becoming a little apprehensive, so assured them that Hastings, even around the docks, was hardly a hotbed of crime and violence, "If Mrs Watson had not spotted me last night, nothing untoward would have happened, I'm sure. The denizens of the inn were a rough-looking lot, but I believe were not ready to pick quarrels, or become too boisterous."

"Let us have a good night's sleep, rise up betimes, and by the time we have driven for four hours or so through some of our picturesque countryside, we shall all be in holiday mood – that is why we are going on this voyage, remember!"

Chapter 13

As had been planned, at about ten minutes to noon, Mr Potter drew up his team on the Hastings wharves, directly across from the *Belle of Sussex*, which was being loaded by a number of seamen and dockworkers. As the passengers descended from the coach, a ship's officer approached and asked for Mr Crabbe, saying, "Captain Kellogg's apologies, sir, he is detained at the dock offices for a moment – I am Arthur Waxman, the first mate. He asked me to check with you what baggage you wished to have loaded, and to make sure that your passengers were conducted to their quarters. I have set aside four cabins for your party, each has two berths – the Captain said that there would be seven or eight of you, is that so?"

"Thank you, Mr Waxman," replied Vincent, "but our two drivers will go with the coach and horses on the French ship, so there will be but six of us travelling in your ship today; two single ladies, who I imagine won't mind sharing, a married couple, and then, finally, this young lad and myself – we two will gladly share as well, won't we, Wilfred? That means that three cabins will suffice – I hope this does not disturb your plans?"

"No, no, sir. That will be no problem at all. Ah, I see the Captain is coming now!"

Captain Kellogg greeted the party cordially and thanked his mate, who saluted and left to continue his other duties. Vincent introduced the Captain to the others, and then asked about the second ship.

"Well, Mr Crabbe, I'm glad to tell you that the harbour master just informed me that Henri is berthing his ship, *Champion Bretonnaise,* right now, at a wharf but a few hundred yards from here. If you wish, as soon as your baggage has been completely taken on board the *Belle*, we can take your coach there, and then talk business with Monsieur Beaumartin. By the way, I heard tell that there was somewhat of a disturbance outside the inn last night; it must have been about the time you were leaving – did you see anything of it?" Vincent just grinned, not wishing to be obliged to relate the whole story.

At the other wharf, the tying up was complete, and Captain Kellogg introduced Vincent to Captain Beaumartin, a small slight fellow, who Vincent thought privately might blow away in any sort of a gale. He was very affable and readily agreed to take the coach and horses to Boulogne, saying that he had other cargo to load also, and would sail the next morning.

"How will you load the coach and horses on board?" asked Vincent, "It seems a daunting task to me – but I am only a landsman!"

"Well, you see, M'sieu, we will make a sort of bridge of timbers laid across from the wharf to the ship – if you look at the rail, you will see that a section of it can be removed. Then we can push and drag the coach across, and lash it down on the deck amidships – we have done this many times, with heavy wagons as well. But the horses are another histoire entirely!"

"So they can't walk across the same bridge?" "Ah, non! Horses are too nervous to walk quietly across such a void, with water below – and if they flinched or jumped they would fall into the harbour! What we do is treat a horse as we do cargo, we use a derrick crane and swing each one across in a sling. Nevertheless, they often get very agitated, poor creatures, and sometimes they are seasick before we ever set sail!"

This gave Vincent an idea; excusing himself, he went over to the team, which was still harnessed to the coach, and stood among them so that all the horses could hear. Then he spoke softly to them in horse language, explaining what was going to happen, and assuring them that they would be safe. Horses are very sensible, and they accepted what he said, and promised to try not become too agitated.

Captain Beaumartin went aboard to give his crew their orders, and soon baulks of timber were being brought from a stack at the back of the wharf. Each needed six men to carry it, and five were put in place until the bridge was wide enough for the coach, which was then unhitched and dragged and pushed across and lashed in place on the deck. Meanwhile the first horse was having a canvas sling put under its belly, the sling then being fastened by stout straps in front of its chest and behind its quarters.

The crew on the lines swung the derrick across from where it was stepped at the foot of the *Champion's* mainmast, and the sling was fastened to four strong ropes running over blocks at the head of the derrick. Then four men, dockworkers or deckhands, heaved on each rope until there was enough height to swing the poor horse across and over the hold of the ship. Finally, they lowered the animal down into the hold, where one of the Woodhampton drivers fussed over it and took it to its stall.

Vincent watched all this, enthralled at the skills displayed, but then thanked Captain Beaumartin and excused himself, "I will see you again in Boulogne, Captain – I must go and board the *Sussex Belle* now or Captain Kellogg will become impatient with me! Thank you and farewell, for the nonce!"

There was a fair wind and the tide was running favourably, so it was not long before the *Sussex Belle* was making good speed out into the channel. Vincent and the rest of the passengers lined the rail and watched the Sussex coast fall away astern of the ship. Then Mr Waxman approached and doffed his hat as he invited the ladies and their companions into the main saloon, where a cold buffet and drinks were laid out for them.

He coughed discreetly and said, "Excuse me for raising the matter, but if there are any amongst you who feel that their stomachs might be uneasy, I would advise them to eat up well! Better to have a full belly than an empty one at sea!"

At this, Euphemia announced that she and Ruprecht had crossed the channel many times, and that it had taken really bad weather to upset them, and that only once or twice, "But today the sea is treating us kindly, I think! Konstanze, do you feel calm? And how about you, young Wilfred?"

"Well, my lady, I feel fine now, but if I start becoming queasy, I shall simply transform myself into a gull or an albatross!"

In the event, the crossing turned out to be very pleasant, and it was late afternoon when the lookout cried out that he could see the buildings of Boulogne. Shortly after that, the companions were bidding farewell to Captain Kellog, Mr Waxman and other key members of the crew.

Beatrice reminded Vincent that they needed accommodation, so the Captain was asked. He recommended two auberges as being suitable for respectable ladies and gentlemen, still quite close to the docks so that they would be conveniently placed for meeting the *Champion Bretonnaise* the next day. At the desk of the first, *L'Auberge de la Manche*, Vincent used his facility in French to secure three comfortable bedrooms, have the valises brought up and check the menu in the fine-looking restaurant.

Chapter 14

It was not the first experience of French cuisine for the twins; they had been accustomed to travelling through France on their way to and from England for many years, while Konstanze had relatives in the East of the country, but Vincent and Beatrice (and, of course, young Wilfred) were intrigued by their dishes, which made much more use of elaborate sauces than they were used to in England. But, let it be said, they all enjoyed their dinners, helped as well by the stimulating effect of sea travel on their appetites!

After dinner, they repaired to a pleasant sitting room where they chatted and sipped wine or cordials and were entertained by a lutenist, a pleasant fellow who, apparently, spent his evenings wandering from establishment to establishment, like an old-time troubadour. He even, having noticed that their conversation was being conducted mainly in German – for Konstanze's comfort – regaled them with a couple of folksongs of that country, for which he was generously rewarded by Ruprecht.

All slept soundly and most of the party needed to be awakened by the staff before enjoying a breakfast in the French style, with fresh crusty bread, ham and cheeses. After a while, Vincent excused himself, explaining that he would go to the docks to see whether the *Champion* had arrived. Ruprecht said he would accompany him, and the two walked down a sloping street to the wharf, where indeed they were just in time to see the French ship being tied up.

Capitaine Beaumartin spotted them from the ship and hailed them, nimbly trotting along a narrow gangplank and coming to greet them and shake their hands. "But I have a little bad news for you!" he said, with a wry grimace, "One of your steeds will need the attention of a farrier before you can proceed, I'm afraid. Apparently he was startled at some time during the night, kicked out at the end of his box, and cast a shoe. Your driver, M. Potter, tells me he was not injured, and could be calmed down quite quickly, but he will need to be re-shod before he can take to the road."

The horse in question was the first to be taken off the ship, again by way of a sling, and Potter led him away from the edge of the wharf, talking quietly to him and soothing him; the farrier, whose shop was not far away, was sent for, and he walked the horse there with little delay, leading him carefully over the cobbles.

Meanwhile another bridge made of heavy baulks of timber was laid to the ship, the coach was manhandled off, and the remaining three horses were lifted off too. Here at Boulogne, there was a tall crane mounted on the dockside, so the ship's derrick was not needed this time.

Vincent and Ruprecht walked back up to the auberge to tell the others what was happening; the farrier had said the work would take him over an hour, by the time he had made a new shoe, trimmed the hoof and fixed it, so Beatrice, Euphemia and Konstanze said they would take a stroll around the town for a little while, accompanied by Ruprecht. Wilfred asked if he could go and watch the farrier at work, so Vincent took him back to the docks, and showed him where to go – it was only a step away.

Mr Potter had gone with his charge to the farrier's shop, and the other driver, Earnshaw by name, had been checking that the coach had sustained no damage during the crossing and the loading and unloading. As well he spent a while grooming the remaining three horses and giving them some feed and water.

Vincent asked a deckhand from the *Champion Bretonnaise* whether M le Capitaine was about, and was taken on board and shown to the captain's cabin. "Well, Capitaine Beaumartin, we ought to conclude our business and settle up; I must say I am very pleased with the service you have given us, and I must also reassure you that I hold neither yourself, nor any of your crew, responsible for our steed's misadventure – horses will be horses!" "Thank you, sir, that is generous of you. Maybe we can repeat our service when you return to England, should you come by this same route."

An agreed sum in gold was tendered and accepted, and the two shook hands on it. "Farewell and again thanks." Said Vincent, "I must now go and see how soon the farrier can restore our steed to us!"

And, as he was descending the gangplank to the dock, along came Potter, leading the horse, with Wilfred riding proudly bareback. As he caught sight of Vincent, Potter said, "I went along to pay the farrier, it was only a modest amount, but the fellow told me that Captain Beaumartin had said that he would cover that cost, so we should consider ourselves fortunate!" "Yes," replied Vincent, "and he will have an even better chance now of serving us again, sensible fellow!"

The horse was harnessed up to the coach with his companions, then the ladies and Ruprecht were fetched from a shop, where they had been accumulating provisions for a substantial picnic luncheon; as they walked to the coach they were followed by a couple of errand boys carrying baskets, which were soon loaded aboard the coach. Before very long the party was making its way onto the main highway to the East.

The day was fair, the road promised to be good, and Euphemia and Konstanze from time to time burst into song, ably accompanied by the reserve driver, Earnshaw, who said he never went anywhere without his flageolet, and proceeded to pipe up a cheerful successions of tunes.

After a couple of hours or so, they espied a meadow by a river, with grassy banks shaded by willow trees. Beatrice cried, "A suitable spot for luncheon, wouldn't you say?" Potter pulled the coach over to the side of the road, and the baskets were carried to a pleasant picnic ground where everyone fell upon the breads, cheeses and ham they had brought, and quenched their thirst with ale and cider.

As they were all congratulating one another on a journey well begun, the sound of hooves was heard on the road, and a pair of horsemen drew up in a cloud of dust by the coach, dismounted, tethered their steeds, and walked toward the picnickers. One seemed to be in charge, as the other fell into step behind him, both with their hands on their sword-hilts.

As they approached, Ruprecht hailed them in French, saying affably, "What ho, to ye, my friends – what is your business with us this fine afternoon?" At that, they both doffed their wide hats and bowed to the ladies, but then, surprisingly, replied in English.

"The business we have," said the leader, "is in the service of Lord Eustace, Ambassador Plenipotentiary of the court of His Majesty, King Arnold of England. Our assigned duty is to make sure that no harm befalls any English subjects, especially members of the nobility. We have been told that a band of Hessians, in league with renegade Englishmen, have kidnapped Lady Beatrice de Gonville, by guile."

Chapter 15

Beatrice held out her hand, so that Vincent could help her up from where she was sitting on the bank. As he did so, she spoke to him quietly; then she approached the men.

"Gentlemen, I am somewhat surprised by what you have just announced. I am indeed the Lady Beatrice de Gonville Musgrave, and my friends here, though certainly Hessian, are in no sense a band. May I introduce Prince Ruprecht of Henzel-Kirschbaum, who is the Landgrave of Hesse, his bride Princess Konstanze, the Landgravine and, lastly, his sister, Princess Euphemia. This other gentleman here is my dear friend of very long standing, Vincent Crabbe and the lad is Wilfred Pemberton, another respected friend. Not one of them is constraining me in any way."

"Now, since I see that, as you must, you have accepted my words as the truth, I have some questions for you in turn – are you prepared to answer?"

The spokesman of the pair was obviously shaken by what he had just heard, but did not attempt to keep his counsel further, saying, with a haughty expression, "Ask away, my lady, we have nothing to hide!"

Beatrice grinned a little at this, in anticipation of his reactions, fixed him with her gaze and asked, "Now, sir, first of all, are you two involved in this enterprise on your own account, or have you been fed this cock-and-bull story to put you up to it? If so, who is hiding behind you, pulling your strings like a puppet-master?"

The man opened his mouth to speak; then his eyed widened and his expression abruptly changed as his words tumbled out unrestrained; he seemed to be hearing what he was saying for the first time.

"You are right, my lady, I know not why I am confessing this, but it is true that we have been recruited by a powerful English nobleman, Lord Bramwell, who claims that his family estates were robbed from him by Lady Louise de Gonville – your mother, I believe, your ladyship – who he also adverts was responsible for the execution of his father, some years ago. I know not whether these claims be true – and I care not, being simply attracted by the fortune he has promised us. He has heard that these estates have been recently gifted to you by your mother, my lady, and it his aim to force you to restore them to him and his family."

"And the talk of Lord Eustace?" asked Beatrice, "More lies, more lies!" said the man, his expression more and more disconsolate with each revelation. His companion, too, was obviously distressed, turning his head this way and that, as though searching for a means of escape; he clasped his leader's arm and spoke to him in low tones.

The spokesman shook himself, stood erect and said, defiantly, "But there is nothing to stop us simply escaping now, we have fast horses, we are armed, and there is nothing you ladies and gentlemen can do about that, whatever you have found out about us! Lord Bramwell is not resident in England; he has not spent any time there since the events I have described – even if you were to interrogate us, we would not be able to tell you anything of his whereabouts, for we simply do not know!"

Beatrice's answer to this was simply to make a gesture toward the coach, next to which the pair had tethered their steeds. To general amazement – but mostly that of the conspirators – it was clear that the horses were no longer there!

"What witchcraft is this?" exclaimed the spokesman, "They were certainly not simply led away, or we would have seen or heard them depart! Was this the work of your coachmen? Well, we shall simply commandeer two of your coach horses, then!"

Ruprecht then said, "Not so fast! You would have to fight us first! You should know that I am an expert swordsman and duelist in the German tradition, that both our coachmen can handle a weapon competently, and that our other friend, who doesn't appear to be here at the moment – I wonder where he might have gone? – is also capable of putting up a fight. I am afraid that you are outnumbered, sir, even if we do not call upon any other of our arcane skills! Be off with you now – we passed a town but two or three leagues back, it should not take you more than three hours to walk there – we shall not trouble ourselves to follow you, and you can then remount yourselves without resorting to violence!"

At this, the second man again pulled at his leader's sleeve and the downcast pair turned and walked back to the road, shoulders slumped.

And then, from behind a group of willow trees on the riverbank, Vincent emerged, with a broad smile on his face.

"As you have probably guessed, I have just now had recourse to dream travel – the stables at Schloss Kirschbaum are now home to two new steeds! Of course, not to put too fine a point on it, it could be said that I am now a horse-thief – I know not whether the penalty for that crime is as severe in France as it is in England, but I feel confident that I shall never be held to account for it!"

All that remained now was to gather up the remains of the picnic, climb aboard the coach, and set off once more, with Wilfred this time singing a rough-hewn ditty that he improvised as he went along, which told of the way in which villains are always brought to book, and just men prevail, to a jaunty accompaniment from Earnshaw's flageolet.

Beatrice, remembering that Euphemia and Ruprecht had followed this carriage route often before, asked them, "Can you recall a likely town where we might put up for the night? I think we should try and settle on a place quite soon; after all our recent excitement I crave a little relaxation, and perhaps some quiet conversation after dinner and a hand or two of piquet or the like to settle our feelings."

Said Ruprecht, "I seem to remember that this highway that we have been following runs through the town of Amiens, which is large enough to offer an ample selection of hostelries. It must not be long before we reach this town – we recently passed through Abbeville, did we not – and then we shall see. It must be five years since I passed this way, but the names of the towns are still impressed in my memory from long before. When I was a young lad, like all young lads I liked to ride on the box with the driver, and he would tell me all about each town as we came to it."

It appeared that Ruprecht's memory had not failed him, as they approached a substantial town and were soon meeting traffic of all descriptions, from coaches down to handcarts, as they joined what must have been a principal thoroughfare leading to the centre. By calling out to other drivers in his rather rough-and-ready French, Potter soon learnt the best way to reach the main square, which was lined with open-air eating establishments and one or two quite grand hotels. Before long the party was being welcomed in the foyer of the most splendid of them.

Chapter 16

It was generally agreed, after a delicious dinner followed by cards and conversation, and following a comfortable night, that it would be pleasant to spend the day exploring Amiens, which seemed as though it might offer some interesting places to visit. So after a satisfying breakfast, the hotel manager was asked to recommend some sights that were worth viewing. Potter and Earnshaw were given the choice of coming with the party or pursuing their own interests; in the event, the two drivers begged to excuse themselves, saying that they would first attend to the horses' needs in the stables of the hotel, and then maybe find a convivial inn, or simply relax somewhere, pointing out that although they had slept well the previous night, they had experienced a poor night on the ship coming over and still needed to catch up on their sleep.

The hotel manager insisted that the group should on no account fail to visit the cathedral, which he claimed was the finest in France, or maybe even in the whole of Europe, so that is where they ventured first. Even young Wilfred was impressed by the architecture and the wonderful sculptures on the face of the high west front, and Princess Konstanze took the opportunity to light a candle in memory of her late mother, while the whole party had no difficulty in wandering around the cathedral and occupying themselves in admiration for more than two hours.

As they left, they were approached by someone in a long habit, who they assumed was a verger, who asked them whether they had enjoyed their tour, and tactfully pointed out the poor box at the entrance.

"Please come again!" he said, as Beatrice dropped a silver coin into the box. "Are you travellers visiting our city? If so, you should take a boat at the quayside yonder and ask the boatman to show you 'les hortilonnages' – these are gardens on small islands by the River Somme, surrounded by canals, and are only reachable by small boat."

Vincent, with Ruprecht, Konstanze and Wilfred, decided to follow up that suggestion and headed for the quayside, which was visible at the end of a street opposite the cathedral square. Beatrice and Euphemia, however, had other plans, which they had hatched up over breakfast; said Beatrice, "We are off to the shops; this is our first town of any size since we came to France, and we must see what latest fashions there are to be found. Of course, it is unlikely that we shall be able to buy any dresses now, but we could certainly order the dressmakers to make dresses for us to collect on our way back!"

"Or we could have them sent on to us in Schloss Kirschbaum!" said Euphemia, getting quite excited at the prospect.

At the quayside, Vincent and his companions found that there were a number of boatmen waiting to be hired. Their craft were equipped only with oars, and their bows were of a rather unusual form, swept up at an angle. After discussing prices and destinations, they engaged a boat with its two rowers, apparently a father and son, and were soon passing along the remainder of the wharves, until the river opened out and they could see a series of islands separated by channels.

The senior boatmen explained that the raked bow was to allow the boat to be driven up on the earthen banks anywhere, so the passengers could go ashore easily. He also asked whether they wished to see flower gardens, vegetable patches or orchards, as all were to be found among these islands. Vincent said that it would be good to buy some fruit, so they were taken to an island where they were welcomed ashore cordially by a pair of elderly women, wearing the traditional clothing of the district, with aprons over long brown shifts, and small bonnets tied under the chin. There were piles of fruit of all kinds set out on sacks on the ground, and the women pressed samples on them, particularly Wilfred, to try. He had no hesitation in biting into a juicy pear, and he was soon followed by the Vincent and the others, who then tried apples, berries and even some chestnuts.

As they were thus engaged, another boat drew near with a large family aboard, parents and at least six girls and boys, with their ages ranging from about eleven down to a babe in arms. The boatman brought his craft in to the bank in the same way as had the first, but before he had run securely up the bank, a little boy of about four or five pushed past his brothers and sisters and made a leap for the shore. In his rush, however, he missed his footing and fell with a splash into the river. His family started off by being amused at this, but soon realised that the child was in difficulties – he splashed about in a panic and then disappeared below the surface; the river was muddy and he could no longer be seen.

The mother and father called out in distress, the mother saying, "We none of us can swim, who can save our son?"

Without a moment's hesitation, Wilfred slipped into the water, becoming at the same time some sort of creature. Only Vincent saw this, for everyone else was intent on trying to look for the child in the river.

In only a minute or so, they all saw a large black dog, streaming with water, emerge from the river, with his teeth clenched around the back of the unfortunate child's trousers. He carried him up the bank, where the father seized him, crying, "Laurent, Laurent, speak to me!" The child coughed and spluttered and then burst into wails of weeping, while his parents fussed over him. Meanwhile, Wilfred, unobserved, regained his normal form.

It was not for several minutes that any member of that family thought to look around for that courageous black dog, but by then, of course, he was nowhere to be found.

The family soon calmed down, the father remarking to Ruprecht and Konstanze, "When you two have children, if you are lucky enough, you will be met with all sorts of drama of this and worse kinds, but, like us, you will never become entirely accustomed to it!"

When Vincent and his companions met them again, back at the hotel, Beatrice and Euphemia were entranced by the tale they were told of this adventure, and could counter it only by relating how they had expended quantities of gold on the commissioning of two ball gowns of the most extravagant design, which they would not describe.

"You will have to wait until they are delivered to Schloss Kirschbaum and we throw the first ball of our stay there!"

Meanwhile, Konstanze slipped into the hotel kitchen where she found the pastry chef and had a few words with him. That evening, at dinner, after the main courses were disposed of, there was a fanfare of trumpets, and the pastry chef, flanked by two of his assistants, bore a large covered platter into the dining room and set it down in front of Wilfred. He was invited to remove the cover and than everyone beheld an amazing three-tier cake, topped by the fondant effigy of a large dog.

Then all joined in a chorus of congratulations for Wilfred's exploit, which caused him to blush and stammer.

Chapter 17

After two eventful days as their introduction to France, the travellers were quite happy that the remainder of their journey across that country was marked by no more than pleasant relaxed driving, sight-seeing and visits to a variety of welcoming hostelries. Wilfred, of course, often begged to be allowed to drive, and both Potter and Earnshaw indulged him, whenever the road was good and the traffic was thin.

The city of Reims was another place that offered many sights of interest, including the impressive cathedral of Notre Dame and vineyards and wineries where they all (save for Wilfred!) enjoyed sampling some of the red wines for which the district was famous.

After a few such enjoyable days, the coach approached a place where the road was crossed by a wooden pole acting as a barrier. As they drew up before it, a soldier emerged from a hut, yawning, and approached the coach. He put his foot on the step and raised himself up so that he could speak to the driver. It was Earnshaw who had the reins at that moment.

"What business have you across this border?" he asked, speaking in English, having apparently recognised the style of the coach and harness, "Who are your passengers and do you have any goods of value?"

Earnshaw, well known by his acquaintances as a plain speaker who brooked no nonsense, replied shortly, "By what authority do you ask these questions?" This caused the soldier to step down and beckon to someone in the hut; a companion then came out to join him, carrying a pike.

"My authority is vested in me in the proper manner, my good man. Since you challenge it so sharply, I am led to wonder whether you might not have something to hide – explain yourself and be quick about it!"

At this, Ruprecht jumped down from the coach and faced the soldier. "I would be obliged, Sir, if you would not harass my driver. I am the Landgrave of Hesse and have every right to approach my own country with my family and friends!" This statement was, of course, accepted for the truth by the soldier, who became a little shame-faced.

Ruprecht continued, "I have heard that men in your position, assigned such a tiresome duty, have sometimes taken the opportunity of exacting a private toll from unwitting travellers. If that was your intention, you chose unwisely. In any case, I demand that you and your companions remove this barrier and allow us to proceed without further delay!" The guard was placated by this and decided to switch to a more ingratiating demeanour. "Yes, of course, your highness, of course. Corporal, pull away the pole, and be quick about it!"

As Ruprecht moved to get back into the coach, the man coughed and said, "Thank you, your honour, for being so reasonable – may I give you a little advice? On the road between here and Frankfurt, if you are intending to travel that way, there have been reports of highwaymen. Only a week since, an open carriage with a lady and gentlemen passed my post coming into France, reporting that they had had a quantity of jewellery and money stolen by such rogues. As I told them at the time, they were lucky, in a way; sometimes if these gentlemen come out of such confrontations empty-handed, they have been known to vent their wrath by damaging the vehicle, or even assaulting the travellers."

As they left the post there was much discussion about this warning. Konstanze became quite fearful, and Beatrice and Euphemia tried to console her, telling her that, first of all, there was no reason to suppose they would be attacked. As Beatrice said, "That guard reported one such instance, a week ago – there must have been many travellers over this road since then. We ourselves have today seen at least thirty carriages or coaches driving in the opposite direction – we waved and greeted them, and none seemed at all distressed to me. And if we are confronted by any such ruffians, we have sufficient resources to deal with them, I am sure, even without resorting to magic!"

"Let us make further enquiries when we stop for the night." said Vincent, "If I know aught, any innkeeper will be full of rumours, and of accounts of what has actually happened on the road recently. Do we know how far it is from this border to a suitable town with a good hotel, Ruprecht? Can you still remember?"

"I must admit that I cannot at the moment, dear Vincent! Let us not fret, however," said Ruprecht, "I do recall that the towns and villages along this highway are not too far apart. We shall just have to see how things progress."

To this, Beatrice and Euphemia, who had been conferring, both started speaking together, then Euphemia waved Beatrice forward, and she announced, "We ladies would like to stop sooner rather than later, there are certain essentials that we can not much longer delay!"

So, within the space of a league or so, a village coming into sight, the coach was drawn up outside what could have been an inn, small though it was. On a bench outside, was a group of elderly men, sitting, chatting and from time to time throwing pebbles half-heartedly into a duck-pond. Vincent hailed them, saying, "Good day, my friends, is this an inn? Can we get a meal and something to drink, perchance?" One of the men got stiffly to his feet and said he would go in and ask, "It will only be peasant fare, you understand, but maybe even you gentry will find that it quells your appetites!"

Meanwhile, the three ladies had vanished behind the building on their errand. When they reappeared, they saw that some dishes had been set out on a rustic table before the inn, and everyone was soon enjoying bread, cheese and speck, with mugs of ale.

The food had been brought by a pair of women, one old and stout and the other young and slender, both wearing aprons over the blouses and full skirts that seemed to be the customary dress of country folk in this district. The younger woman, too shy to speak to the adults, asked Wilfred if he would like an apple, which he gratefully accepted, thanking her and asking her name and the name of the village. "They call me Gisela," she answered, "but this place has no real name, we just call it the village. There is a real town a half hour away by walking, which is called Oberstein. There is a big inn there, and if you want, they will be able to put you all up for the night, I shouldn't wonder. We have no room here for guests, this little inn is mainly just a place for the farm workers to drink beer."

Appetites satisfied, Vincent paid the modest amount asked and the party took again to the coach, calling out their thanks and farewells to the villagers. It was Earnshaw's turn to drive; he and Potter had made sure that the horses, unharnessed one by one, had drunk their fill at the duck-pond.

Chapter 18

Before long they came to the town of Oberstein, perched over a river gorge and surrounded by rocky crags. The highway took them to a square at the town centre, where they saw a large inn or small hotel. They pulled up outside, and Vincent went inside to see whether they could be accommodated for the night. He soon re-emerged, announced that he had booked some rooms and told the drivers that there was a stable-yard by the side of the building where they could have the horses watered and fed and stabled for the night. Then everyone disembarked, leaving their valises for the hotel staff to deal with.

The hotel was not as elaborate as the one in Amiens, but comfortable enough. They were all made welcome by the proprietor, a tall imposing figure with whiskers. He ushered them into the dining room and soon a waiter came to ask them what they wished to order.

Beatrice asked him, "Does this region have any special dishes? If so, please tell us about them, for we are anxious to sample as many examples of new fare as we can while we are travelling." The waiter brightened up and said, "Well, my lady, if you will still be here for the evening meal tomorrow, you should certainly try our local *Schwenkbraten*, but for that you will have to join our other guests in the gardens behind the hotel, for it is traditionally cooked outdoors over an open fire in a pit, does that sound attractive to you?"

Beatrice clapped her hands and said, "Very good, we shall look forward to that! I think we are all ready for a meal right now, so what can you offer us for dinner this evening?"

The waiter said they should leave it to him, and offered them some bread to nibble while they waited. Very soon, two serving maids brought soup, more breads and salads, and everyone conversed happily while they were waiting for the main course, which they were pleased to find comprised large whole baked fish, fresh from the river, they were told, followed by a wonderful selection of pastries and cakes.

The proprietor came over, asking them if everything was satisfactory, saying, "If you ladies and gentlemen are intending to stay in our town for a day or two, we have some interesting places to visit, such as the famous church on the rocks, and the gemstone workshops. Just come and ask me when you are ready to go out, and I will tell you more. Please enjoy your meal; Eckhardt tells me that you will be joining us at the *Schwenker* tomorrow evening; did he tell you there would be singing and folk-dancing, there, too?"

After dinner, they all settled down in comfortable chairs in a sitting room, where they made conversation with other guests, among them a family from Bohemia, on their way to Paris. The son of this family, a youth of about fifteen, was soon engaged in a friendly competition with Wilfred, each describing the interesting places they had visited and what they had done there and trying to top the other's tales. Vincent was half-aware of this conversation, of which he heard snatches during breaks in his own chat with the youth's father, and he was a little perturbed when he heard Wilfred trying to score points by boasting of the fact that he was travelling with nobility, the Landgrave and Landgravine of Hesse prominent among them. Vincent made a mental note that he would take Wilfred aside later and remonstrate with him about these indiscretions.

Euphemia and Konstanze found themselves talking to a pair of sisters from the town, who explained that they often visited the hotel for dinner, and then would play cards with friends afterwards, "But our card partners are out of town, visiting relatives, so we shall just have to be content with conversation!"

"Not necessarily!" said Euphemia, "If you are prepared to put up with a gentleman, my brother Ruprecht is a keen player also, as is Konstanze here, his wife. We may not know the games you prefer, so you will have to be patient with us!"

This offer was happily taken up, and soon all five people were enjoying the play, taking turns to sit out, as the games they were shown mostly called for four players. Beatrice and Vincent preferred just to talk with the other guests, and Vincent soon discovered a fellow bee-keeper, so the two spent the rest of the evening sharing their professional lore, while leaving Beatrice to talk about music with a lady who told her she had a spinet bought in Kasselburg – but not from Master Steiglitz – so that they too were soon exchanging snippets of information.

Everybody was ready to fall into bed that night, but awoke the next day feeling fresh and eager to see the sights. As he had promised, Herr Winkel, the proprietor, described the local attractions, including the renowned (he said) church on the rocks and the local industry of lapidary or gem cutting.

"The mountains here are full of natural caves, and in those caves can be found rock crystals and many semi-precious stones which, when cut and polished, reveal beautiful figurations. The gem-cutters use polishing wheels driven by water, so their workshops are mainly perched on the edge of the gorge – the young gentleman in particular will be very interested to see them work, I'm sure!"

After the steep climb up the mountainside to the famous church, which was indeed almost hanging on a precipitous rocky slope, they were all ready for a snack, and then visited two or three gem-cutters' workshops, where not only were they fascinated to watch and admire the artisans' skills, but also bought a number of samples, some which were suitable as pendants and brooches, others which were meant to be inlaid into furniture.

After all that, most of the party decided to retire to their chambers to rest themselves and get ready for the *Schwenker* feast. When the time arrived, Eckhardt the waiter called at each bedroom, and told them that they should descend to the garden.

As they went down the steps behind the hotel, they were greeted by the sight of a multitude of flickering lanterns hanging from the trees and the sounds of a German band, with brass instruments high and low, tambourines and lusty singing.

There was already quite a throng in the garden, many of them standing around the cooking-pit, watching the cooks tending to the log fire and preparing the meats, mainly cuts of pork and beef that had been marinated in oils and spices, for cooking.

The smells were enough to give anyone an appetite, but Beatrice and her friends were in no need whatsoever of any such encouragement, and waited impatiently on a row of benches for the cooks and the waiters to perform their duties.

And, once served, they set to with a will, finding the meats and accompanying vegetables and salads as good a feast as they had enjoyed for many a month. Before the eating was over, a troupe of folk-dancers, in the traditional dress of the region, entertained them with a succession of lively formation dances. All agreed that it had been an excellent evening!

Chapter 19

As they took their leave of Herr Winkel after breakfast, Beatrice remembered to ask him about highwaymen.

"We are headed for Frankfurt, and thence for Schloss Kirschbaum, but we can choose a different way if necessary. The crossing-guard told us the other day that the Frankfurt road has seen the activities of highwaymen – have you heard aught of these ruffians?"

"Well, my lady," he replied, looking serious, "there have certainly been some accounts of that nature, but I know not how likely it be that you might encounter any such rogues. But, with us in the inn today is someone who will be able to tell us more, since he is a regular traveler on that road. If it please you, my lady, I will take you to him – he is having breakfast at this moment."

Beatrice and Vincent went with the innkeeper into the main dining room. They were led to a table where two men of military appearance were seated. Herr Winkel bowed to one of them, saying, "Oberst Grossman, I'm sorry to disturb you, may I introduce Lady Beatrice de Gonville Musgrave and Herr Crabbe. Their party is driving to Frankfurt, and they have heard tell of highwaymen on the road, and I thought you might be able to provide them with fresh intelligence on this matter."

Oberst Grossman rose to his feet, clicked his heels and bowed as he took Beatrice's hand to kiss it. "Good morning, my lady, and to you, Sir!" and he shook Vincent's hand. "Please sit down with us and I will tell you what I know. Will you take something to drink while I do so? It will not take me very long."

Beatrice sat opposite to him and Vincent opposite his companion, who also rose to his feet and introduced himself, "Hauptmann Anders, at your service."

Oberst Grossman explained, "My assistant and I are charged with patrolling the highways in this Land, and we have only yesterday ridden from the French border. I can tell you that, while we did hear of an incident of daylight robbery a week or so since, in which a French family heading for home had jewels and money stolen, we have come across nothing more over the last few days. In my experience, such attacks are commonly perpetrated at dusk and in isolated areas. We always advise travelers to set out early and make sure to reach their destinations in full daylight. At this time of year, of course, this is no real restriction, since the evenings are long. Unfortunately, we can, of course, offer no absolute guarantee of safety since these robbers are unpredictable in their habits."

Hauptmann Anders raised his hand to speak, "Herr Oberst, would it not be possible for us to time our return to Frankfurt such that we will be riding ahead or after these travelers?"

"Very good, Anders! Well said – of course we can. We have to make some visits to officials in this town first, but will in any case be setting out for Frankfurt in no more than an hour. If, my lady, you and your party set out in your coach now, we shall pass you on the road fairly soon. Would that make you feel safer?"

"That is very good of you, Oberst Grossman. Although we are not particularly fearful for ourselves, we are travelling with the Landgrave and Landgravine of Hesse, and the young Landgravine in particular will be reassured to know of your close attention."

The two officers rose and clicked their heels again as Beatrice and Vincent left. They thanked Herr Winkel for his help and went out to the coach, which was all loaded and ready to set off.

Konstanze, of course, was very glad to hear about the conversation with the patrol, asking, "When do you think we might approach Frankfurt?" Ruprecht said he would check with the drivers next time they stopped, but guessed that it would be no later than early evening, everything going well.

The day was again fine, the road, though rocky in places, was in fairly good repair, and the coach made excellent speed. They met several carriages and single horsemen, and as usual, waved and greeted them as they passed, getting cheerful replies.

After a couple of hours, everyone, especially Beatrice, started thinking about luncheon, and Potter and Earnshaw were asked to keep their eyes open for a suitable establishment in the next town or large village that they reached. As they started to descend into a wooded valley, they heard the sound of hoof-beats, and Oberst Grossman and his troop, Hauptmann Anders and five other riders, drew level with the coach. The Oberst waved his hat cheerfully as they passed and carried on into what could now be seen was a township sited on a smallish river.

The coachmen drew up by the small green square in the centre, where there were several establishments that looked to be likely eating places. All the passengers climbed down, stretching their legs and backs. Herr Grossman's men were already watering their steeds at horse-troughs by the green, and the Oberst came over and greeted the travelers, saying, "Well, my ladies and gentlemen, we have seen nothing untoward on the road so far, I'm glad to report. But later on, we shall be keeping especially watchful as we approach the outskirts of Frankfurt itself."

Beatrice thanked him for this reassurance and invited him and Hauptmann Anders to join them for luncheon, but the soldier gracefully declined, bowing and clicking his heels once again, saying, "We have a regular eating-place a little further down the road which is used to dealing with the appetites of we rough soldiery! But many thanks for your gesture, we may well see you all before Frankfurt."

Luncheon was taken in a popular eating-house, crowded with local people, and was, as usual devoured avidly by the party, who were all finding that coach travel was good for the appetite!

In an hour, however, they were ready to proceed, and soon the horses were labouring somewhat as the road out of the township climbed the other side of the river valley. In fact, Potter, who was driving at the time, pulled up at a flat spot in the road and asked his passengers whether they were willing to get out and walk a little, to spare the horses. Of course, everyone was indeed willing, and started to wander along the grassy sides of the road, which was passing through woodland.

Wilfred, whose energy seemed to be inexhaustible, darted off along various paths into the woods, returning with bunches of wildflowers, which he presented, blushingly, to the ladies. But one such excursion seemed to Vincent to be taking rather too long, and he remarked to the others, half seriously, "I hope our young friend has not fallen down or met a bear!" At this, Ruprecht ventured into the edge of the wood and started whistling and calling out "Wilfred, Wilfred, where are you, lad?"

Chapter 20

After he had walked some yards into the woods, Ruprecht was rather relieved to catch sight of Wilfred, who ran up to him, somewhat flushed and excited, and stammered, "I have discovered a band of robbers, I think! I nearly stumbled upon them, but fortunately was able to draw back before I was sighted!"

Said Ruprecht, "Slowly, slowly, lad! Let us go and tell the others all about this and explain why you believe them to be robbers."

At the road, everyone gathered around Wilfred, who was now rather calmer. He took a drink from a flask of water that Konstanze had with her, and started his account.

"Well, I was just trotting along the path, looking this way and that and trying to see if there were any berries to pick, when I came to the edge of a glade. There was a fire lighted in a ring of stones, and around it, seated on logs with the grass growing up around as though this was a regular camp, were half-a-dozen or so roughly-dressed men, gnawing on pieces of meat that they had apparently been cooking, quaffing mugs of ale and laughing and shouting. I might have taken them for simple woodcutters but for the sight of a lady and gentleman, seated on the ground back to back, bound together with ropes and gagged and blindfolded!"

This news caused much consternation in the group, especially for Konstanze, who started wringing her hands and breathing heavily. Beatrice calmed her, saying, "We can deal with this, my dear, there is no need to be too concerned – we will walk up to the coach and then we shall be four strong men and three ladies – enough to deal with any half-a-dozen villains! Besides, we should not forget Oberst Grossman and his men!"

"So, Wilfred, if you have settled yourself, please become a bird and fly ahead to find them – Herr Grossman said that they would soon be stopping at their regular eating place, which cannot be too far ahead. But, before you leave on this mission, I think you need another two arcane gifts. Please come here and close your eyes, and I will take your hands."

Beatrice murmured some words quietly and then said, "Open your eyes, Wilfred. I have just given you the gift of veracity, so that when you speak to Oberst Grossman you have only to look into his eyes and he will believe you without question. I have also given you the gift of language, so you may speak to him in German, although his English is quite serviceable. Now become a bird and fly off until you find the troopers. Maybe you should regain human form out of their sight – they will be astonished enough at your message. We shall stay here with the coach."

It was less than half an hour before those waiting by the coach heard the hoof-beats of the troop approaching, and then the riders came into sight, Oberst Grossman at their head, and Wilfred riding pillion to Hauptmann Anders. Further explanations were made and it was decided that Ruprecht should accompany the soldiers on foot into the woods, Wilfred acting as guide, while Vincent and the two drivers stayed with the ladies as protection.

The patrol tried to move as quietly as possible through the trees, and soon heard sounds of revelry ahead; as Wilfred had reported, the path led to an open glade. By this time, two or three of the robbers were already overcome by drink and were dozing on the grass, leaning on the logs they had been using as seats, while the others continued laughing and boasting. Some soldiers skirted behind the group, walking through the trees, and then Oberst Grossman and Anders stepped forward, swords upraised, and accosted the villains, who immediately put up their hands in surrender.

One burly member of the band leapt to his feet and tried to run, but he was soon brought down and pinned by two of the soldiers, who manacled his hands behind his back – the soldiers carried pairs of manacles dangling from their belts, and were well drilled in their use, and it took but a few minutes before all the robbers were manacled also and led away to the road. "We will march them to the city!" announced Hauptmann Anders.

While the soldiers were doing all this, Ruprecht went to the couple tied together on the ground. He first removed their gags and blindfolds, and they blinked and looked around, still dazed. He reassured them that they were now safe, and, helped by Wilfred, freed them from their bonds and helped them to their feet. They staggered at first, so he led them to sit on a log, where they started rubbing their arms and ankles to restore the circulation.

Ruprecht then introduced himself as the Landgrave of Hesse, whereupon the gentleman responded, saying, "I thank you most sincerely for rescuing us. I am Graf Wilhelm von Wilderswil, a resident of Switzerland, and this is my wife, Lady Sybilla. We were travelling to Frankfurt to set up a new business, when we were suddenly waylaid by these wretches. I know not what has become of our carriage, our driver, my secretary and my wife's maid. We were also carrying gold and other valuables – all gone, now, I suppose."

Oberst Grossman then introduced himself, and assured the Graf that he was in good hands now, and that he would inform the authorities in Frankfurt. "Meanwhile," he said, "come with me and the Landgrave Ruprecht to the highway and we shall meet the others of his party, make you comfortable and take you into the city."

With Grossman in attendance, the coach and its passengers were soon approaching the outskirts of the city of Frankfurt. Once inside the main town gate, the Oberst led them to a barracks building, explaining that he would report the recent events to his commander and set in train an attempt to track down the Graf's carriage and his servants.

When he emerged, he had his horse led away, and took his place on the box of the coach, saying he would direct the party to a hotel that he knew well and could heartily recommend.

"Once you are all settled," he said to Graf Wilhelm, "I will take notes of the details of your carriage and all your goods, and the names and descriptions of your retinue, and we shall soon have agents enquiring in all quarters of the city. We have, as well as our soldiers, an efficient municipal constabulary, and there is also a network of informers, including some rather dubious characters, who between them miss very little of what goes on in the lower reaches of our fine city! There is one in particular who I have found in the past can provide valuable information on stolen goods – at a price, of course!"

"I will call on you in the morning, but meanwhile, please settle yourselves down for a splendid meal, an enjoyable evening of exchanging experiences, and a comfortable and restful night's sleep! Please assure yourselves, ladies and gentlemen, that I always appreciate the opportunity to exercise my skills as a fighter against criminals of all complexions! Good night, all!"

Chapter 21

The proprietor of the hotel welcomed the party with open arms, and soon found them four large rooms on an upper floor that promised to be very comfortable. Since the Graf and Grafine von Wilderswil had lost all their luggage, and the outfits they had on were looking rather the worst for wear, because of the distressing experiences the couple had been through, Ruprecht and Konstanze offered to lend them some of their clothing until they could buy replacements or have their own returned.

Nevertheless, an hour or so later, they were all ready to take their seats in the dining room and sample the extensive menu on offer. During the meal, life histories and accounts of recent adventures were exchanged, and it became apparent that all of them would soon become close friends. After dinner they settled down in a comfortable sitting room and continued their conversations until, quite early in the evening, Sybilla excused herself and her husband, saying that the excitement of the day had left them feeling weary.

Next morning, all feeling refreshed, they met over breakfast and were continuing their lively chatting, even the normally shy Wilfred, who seemed to have been given some confidence by his part in the adventure, when Oberst Grossman and the faithful Anders came into the room.

They went round the table, greeting each of the party with the customary clicking of the heels, and then Grossman suggested that, if everyone had finished breakfast, they might adjourn to a separate sitting room, since their business was private. Once they were all seated, he announced, "I have some successes and some failures to report. First, my dear Graf von Wilderswil, your carriage has been found! These ruffians must be unused to any more than petty thievery, because two of them approached a respectable livery stable here in Frankfurt, and attempted to persuade the owner to purchase the carriage, without any idea of its worth, or thinking that he might wish to know how they had acquired it. While engaging them in conversation, he quietly had one of his staff go and tell the constables, and very soon these two miscreants were in custody and being searchingly interrogated! They will, of course, also be grilled to find where the driver and your other staff might be. I sincerely hope they have come to no harm."

"I should let you know that I have sent word to the man of whom I spoke yesterday, who has an entry into many of the criminal groups of our city. Like any other large city, Frankfurt has an underworld whose members range from out-and-out villains to those whose eye is on the main chance, even if it requires them to betray their companions on occasion. I expect a reply from this man soon, because he knows that I have the power to grant him concessions. Herr Anders will tell you next about his visit to the constabulary depot."

Hauptmann Anders then told of his enquiries, admitting that no information of note had yet emerged, but saying that the constables were usually able to extract useful facts by persistent firm questioning.

While he was talking, a soldier appeared at the door, beckoning Grossman, who went over to speak to him, nodding his head and then breaking into a smile. "Well done, Tinkermann, please show them in!" The soldier saluted, then stood aside and ushered in two men and a woman, walking slowly and rather wearily. When Wilhelm and Sybilla saw them, they exclaimed that they were happy and relieved to see them well, shook hands or embraced each of them, and led them to sit down on a couch.

Beatrice went to ask hotel staff to bring refreshments, and after a few minutes rest and recovery the three were ready to tell their stories.

When their carriage had been stopped, the robbers had tied up and blindfolded the Graf and his wife, and then done the same to the driver, Franz Müller, the secretary, Felix Strasser, and Sybilla's French maid, Ernestine Fournelle, who were then bundled into the carriage. One of the band than drove the carriage out to a wooded part of the country, where the three captives were abandoned.

They managed to untie one another and found their way to a road, where, eventually, a farmer took pity on them and took them to his village on the outskirts of Frankfurt. From there they managed, after losing their way once or twice, to make their way on foot to the city and present themselves at the constabulary post.

At first, their story was received with some scepticism, but eventually a constable put two and two together and contacted the barracks where Grossman and Anders are stationed.

"Well, well!" said Grossman, "We are doing quite well so far, but finding the valuables might be a more difficult task. If I know aught, the robbers will have disposed of the goods in varied ways. I am sure that the constables will be approaching those disreputable establishments that deal in second-hand clothing and, of course, we have a list of those who handle stolen jewellery, but it is never very easy to track down gold. All we can hope for is that some of the missing items might still be held together, not yet passed on."

"Tell me, Graf von Wilderswil, how were you carrying your valuables and gold? Were they in chests?"

Wilhelm answered, "We had dispersed those items throughout the valises with our clothes, thinking that they would be safer that way from being purloined. My wife's most valuable jewels were in a sharkskin case, but that, too, was in a valise among clothing. It all depends, I suppose, how diligently these thieves examined the luggage, and whether they were able to find these items."

Vincent raised his hand at this point. "If the jewellery and gold were kept for some time in the valises with clothing, then a tracking dog with a keen nose might be able to detect traces of their scent, even if they have been separated. We have access to such a tracking dog, a beagle, what is called in German a Spürhund." He looked unobtrusively towards Wilfred, who, quick on the uptake, nodded slightly.

The Oberst nodded, but said, "Of course, we must first find the valises. I take it that they were of high quality, is that so?" Sybilla replied, "Oh yes, they were a set of a dozen, of different sizes, but all of the same kind, made of horse-hide dyed a deep burgundy, with our family coat of arms embossed in gold upon them. They are unmistakable!"

"Strangely enough," said Oberst Grossman, "this makes our task easier. Any disreputable dealer would think twice about taking such distinctive items, whereas more commonplace goods might be accepted with little question. We must simply wait for reports from the constables; I shall pass on the details you have given me, together with any distinguishing features of the contents of the valises. And we need the amount and denomination of any gold coins. Of course, a clever thief would put stolen goods away for a while until the hue and cry abates; but I do not believe we are dealing with clever thieves!"

Chapter 22

Vincent had been thinking along similar lines, and then said, "When the group of villains was apprehended in the forest, they were gathered around a fire and seated, as Wilfred noticed, on logs around which the grass had grown up, as though it might be a regular camp for them. What if they have some hut or other more permanent building near by? They may have concealed their ill-gotten gains there, and since we surprised them, may not have had any further chance to dispose of the goods. Why do we not go there, Wilfred included, and make a search?"

This idea appealed to Grossman, who said, "We should take some of my men, too, lest they have left a watchman guarding their loot, and perhaps Graf von Wilderswil would like to accompany us to identify his possessions, should any be found."

"Certainly!" replied Wilhelm, "and we can travel in our carriage, since it has been recovered – but, wait, do we know whether our horses are still with it, or have these ruffians sold them separately?"

"I will make enquiries!" said Grossman, "But if we need to find fresh horses, the livery stable proprietor will be able to supply them; the carriage is still in his yard, as far as I know. I and my men will ride our own steeds, and then, if pursuit is called for, we shall be ready for it."

At this point, Beatrice, who had been talking with Euphemia, Konstanze and Sybilla, announced that, while that expedition was in train, she and Euphemia would take a carriage to the shop of Fritzi and Clotilda, "I know not whether our friends will be there at the moment, but in any case it will be pleasant to see their Frankfurt establishment for the first time, and to speak with the manageress, Frau Gluck, who, we have been told, is a very intelligent and entertaining person. Konstanze and Sybilla will stay here in the hotel, to wait for any news that Oberst Grossman's men or the constables might have discovered."

Within the hour, the carriage and horsemen approached the spot where the encounter with the robbers had taken place. Herr Müller, who had insisted on driving, although he was still quite weary, stayed with the carriage, accompanied by one of the soldiers. Then Wilfred led Vincent, Ruprecht and Wilhelm to the glade. There were still embers smouldering in the fireplace, and there were bones and beer-mugs scattered around it.

As well as the path by which they had approached, there seemed to be three or four others, looking as though they had been used to different degrees. Wilfred tried one, but then came back, holding a kerchief to his nose and saying, "We need not go that way; it is clear that the dell down there has been used only as a latrine!" The next two paths they tried simply dwindled away to nothing among the trees, so Vincent suggested they try a different approach. Warning the Oberst and his men that they were about to behold something unusual, and that they should keep the sight to themselves if they could, he asked Wilfred if he would become a beagle, and then try to pick up a scent trail.

He made the transformation, to a chorus of surprised comments, from Wilhelm as well as from the soldiers, and then snuffled and sniffed around the logs, and also at the discarded mugs, but at first did not seem to find any trail of note. Then, as he started along the entrance pathway, Vincent remarked, "Of course! This path must have often been used by the band; let us see whether it branches off before the highway."

And, sure enough, after a few yards, Wilfred barked twice and set off through a gap in a clump of bushes, the others following. It took a few minutes, as they had to hold aside branches hanging low over the path, but then they emerged into a clear grassy area bounded by a high rocky cliff. And visible at the base of the cliff were the dark entrances of two caves, with low roofs, but still passable for a man. Outside one of them was a small pile of fire-blackened branches.

Wilfred regained his own shape and said, "I did not feel I should run into either of these caves as a beagle, in case the thieves have left a guard behind; but maybe if I became a small creature, perhaps a rat, no notice would be taken of me and I could see what the caves hold, if anything. Besides, a rat, being a nocturnal creature, with eyes suitable for dark places, would not need the use of a torch."

Vincent was pleased at this idea – he had always taken Wilfred as a clever and resourceful boy – and he and the others encouraged him to proceed as he had suggested.

In the form of a rat, he first disappeared into the cave that had no remains of torches by its entrance, and soon emerged, shaking his head. He then ran into the second cave, this time taking several minutes before he re-emerged. Becoming Wilfred again, he reported, "There was no-one in either cave, in fact there was nothing at all in the first, and there were no footprints on its sandy floor, so I do not believe it has been used for any purpose. But in the second, there were footprints a-plenty, and scrape marks as though something heavy had been dragged in there. And, I am happy to relate that, at the end of the cave, half concealed by piles of branches, I saw some valises! I could not count them, because they were stacked one before the other, but there seemed to be more than three or four!"

Vincent and the others were joyful at this, clapping each other on the shoulders and grinning broadly. Oberst Grosman instructed two of his soldiers to take some of the blackened branches back to the camp-site and see whether they could reignite them from the embers for use as torches. When they returned they cautiously entered the cave and within a few minutes returned, each dragging a valise, which indeed were of a burgundy colour and bore the Wilderswil coat of arms.

The soldiers went back in, and at the end had retrieved nine valises, all of them securely strapped up and apparently undisturbed, as well as a stout chest that was not recognized by the Graf. Wilhelm anxiously rummaged through the contents of the cases and found that there seemed to be nothing missing – there was gold there, still in its leathern bags. As he said, it seemed that the robbers had not had the chance to examine these valises. But the sharkskin case with Sybilla's favourite jewels was not to be found. Said Wilhelm, "I cannot be sure which valise it was in – it may well be that it was in one of the three that are still unaccounted for. But I am very pleased at having recovered the nine that we have here!"

Very soon, everything had been taken to the carriage, but then Vincent said, "We should not assume that what we have found so far were the only spoils hidden by the robbers; what might be a good notion is for a couple of your men, Oberst, to stay and look round and then hide somewhere near to intercept any thief who might return." Grossman assented readily to this.

Chapter 23

When they had arrived back at the hotel, Graf Wilhelm went inside and invited Sybilla and Konstanze to come down to the stable-yard, where the carriage was being unloaded, to show them what had been discovered. Sybilla, of course, was overjoyed to see that nine of the valises had been retrieved, and quickly unstrapped and opened one or two more of them, to confirm whether Wilhelm was right in supposing that they had not been opened by the robbers. She then said, "I am a little puzzled why they took these particular valises, and ignored the other three. They were the smaller ones, it is true, but why would they not take them as well? Those were the ones we put under the seats of the carriage – oh, oh! – Wilhelm my dear! Has anyone thought to check under the seats?"

Wilhelm exclaimed and struck his forehead with his open hand, and he and Sybilla sprang into action, climbing into the carriage and lifting the cushioned covers that formed the front and rear seats. And there, completely undisturbed, lay the three missing valises, stitched up in sackcloth to keep out the dust!

While everyone was standing around congratulating each other, Beatrice and Euphemia drew up in their hackney carriage accompanied by none other than Fritzi and Clotilda, and so, after a round of introductions, they, too had to be told the good news. Said Beatrice, "Well, well, it very much appears that we now have an excellent excuse for a celebratory luncheon! Let us all go to the dining room and see what this splendid hotel can provide for us – good Rhenish wine is called for, I do believe!"

Over the meal there was much chatter, what with more introductions and everyone being brought up to date. Fritzi explained that she and Clotilda had dream travelled from Hastings to Frankfurt only the previous evening, and related the account of how they had engaged a male manager and a saleswoman for the Hastings shop; on this occasion, since they were newly possessed of the gift of veracity, and had also sought advice from Master Samuel and recommendations from the constabulary, they were quite confident that their new staff would be found trustworthy and efficient.

Sybilla was particularly interested to hear that these two ladies were successfully running three silverware establishments, in three separate cities, saying, "My husband Wilhelm and I have come here to Frankfurt to set up another branch of our own business – we have a successful concern in our home town of Zurich, where we deal in clocks and watches, and we are intending to add to it here. This is a modern trade – not long ago clocks were only to be found in churches and public buildings, but now well-to-do folk want them for their own houses, and some very rich people are prepared to pay a high price for a pocket watch. My husband will show you!"

Wilhelm was easily persuaded to do this, taking from his pocket a wash-leather bag from which he carefully removed an object the shape and size of a pear, crafted in gold. He pressed a catch, and a cover sprang open to reveal the dial, marked out in hours and minutes, but with only a single hand, proudly remarking, "There you are, ladies and gentlemen, as you can clearly see, the time is one hour after noon, or close to that!"

Clotilda asked him, "Do you make these clocks and watches in your establishment?" "No, no, we buy them from skilled craftsmen, most of whom work as one-man enterprises, or with an apprentice or a single assistant; these artificers mostly prefer to concentrate on the designing and production of their clocks and watches, and are very pleased to leave the commercial aspects of the business to us. We have not yet had the chance to look for any premises in Frankfurt, since we were somewhat rudely interrupted – perhaps you noticed! – so, if you and Fritzi are willing to help us, we would be grateful for advice about a good location and the choice of a shop, and it also sounds as though you two ladies would be a great help in finding and interviewing suitable staff. We shall run it ourselves for a while, but we want to keep Zurich as our headquarters, and to leave Frankfurt to be run by a manager."

Sybilla added, "And, of course, we would like to make enquiries about clockmakers working in this area. We shall speak to any merchants already engaged in this trade in Frankfurt – we have no wish to stir up rivalries, but in a city of this size, serving an extensive area, there must be room for several merchants of our kind."

Fritzi had been listening with great interest and added, "I have been thinking that the customers for clocks and watches must be similar in some respects to our own clients for silverware – prosperous families and the nobility – so we could each support the other's business. This is all beginning to sound very encouraging and exciting!"

As the company was moving into the adjacent sitting room, to sip some more wine and continue talking, Hauptmann Anders came into the hotel, approached Grossman and drew him aside. They conversed quietly and earnestly for a few minutes, then Anders exclaimed, "That is excellent news, sir! So has everything been recovered?"

Grossman replied, "Even better – we have recovered a chest as well, which is not part of the von Wilderswil goods. We have not yet opened it, it is securely locked, and there are no marks on it suggesting that the thieves have attempted to open it, either. Is there any word among our acquaintances in the alleyways as to other members of the band? We seemed to have apprehended only the lower ranks, so I would not be surprised to find that they were led by a man or men considerably less stupid that they!"

"No word yet, Herr Oberst, apart from one or two conjectures that have yet to be followed up," said Anders, "but I shall ask one of my comrades to talk again to the constables this afternoon." He clicked his heels, saluted Grossman, bowed politely in the direction of the others, and left the hotel.

"Now," said Oberst Grossman, "I must take my leave of you, ladies and gentlemen. Although this gathering is all very pleasant, I have my duties to perform. I shall leave this affair in the capable hands of the soldiery and the constables, and then Anders and our men will take horse once more and set out for the remaining towns on our circuit. I have asked one of my esteemed colleagues, the deputy chief constable, Herr Feinstein, to come and see you so you may ensure that he is comprehensively briefed and that there are no more matters that might need his attention. I must not forget, either, to arrange that those of my soldiers who have been keeping watch at the robbers' camp are relieved. They have not made any discoveries, or I would have been told of them. Farewell, ladies and gentlemen all – I shall have the pleasure of seeing you again, I am sure!"

He went round the company, kissing the ladies' hands and shaking those of the gentlemen, clicking his heels on each occasion. As for Wilfred, he patted him on the head, saying with a grin, "Good dog!" Wilfred was not at all offended at this!

Chapter 24

After Oberst Grossman had taken his leave, everybody discussed what would be done to continue their travels. Beatrice and her companions decided that it was too late to set off that day. "Besides," said Beatrice, "the meals offered by this hotel are too good to miss! Let us enjoy a good dinner and then take carriage for Schloss Kirschbaum tomorrow morning. Ruprecht, how long is the drive, do you recall?"

"Oh, in good weather like we are enjoying now, no more than five or six hours, as long as we are not held up by highwaymen!"

"Please don't joke!" exclaimed Konstanze, "I am still a little nervous, and the good Oberst and his men will not be accompanying us on our road this time!"

Fritzi and Clotilda said that they would stay in Frankfurt for a few more days, to settle any outstanding business and select a few items to send to Hastings, but would join the others in Schloss Kirschbaum when they had done with that. And Clotilda was going to spend some time with her son Karsten, who was in the upper class of his school in Frankfurt, boarding with his Tante Irmalinda, his late father's sister, and thinking about what he should do next.

Then Fritzi had a thought and asked the von Wilderswils, "Would you two like to come and see our silverware shop, once you have settled yourselves and checked all your belongings? We could talk about finding premises for you and even look at some suitable locations, and you could also think about hiring staff. We have been in business here for over ten years, so we are familiar with the way that commerce is conducted here in Frankfurt and we are on good terms with many of the local business proprietors."

Wilhelm and Sybilla were very taken with this suggestion and readily fell in with it. Fritzi told them the address of their shop, saying that it was within easy walking distance, so they should not bother with taking their carriage. "And as well," she said, "this will give you a chance to become familiar with the commercial quarter of this city."

"Could I bring along my secretary, Felix Strasser?" asked Wilhelm, "I would like him to make notes and acquaint himself with some aspects of business in Frankfurt, too." Fritzi and Clotilda were happy for him to do this, of course.

Over dinner, the conversation ranged from business to family affairs, and Ruprecht and Euphemia said that maybe Karsten would like to spend some holiday time with them at Schloss Kirschbaum, now that he was finishing with school.

While they were talking, a young woman, dressed neatly but plainly, came over and spoke to Ruprecht, saying, "Forgive me for eavesdropping, sir, but I could not but overhear that you are setting out for Schloss Kirschbaum in the morning. My name is Angela Sonderhoff, and my dear departed Mama was for a time lady's maid to the Countess Roswitha, your aunt, sir, and I used to visit the castle from time to time. I am approaching you in the hope that I might be able to beg a ride with you back to Schloss Kirschbaum tomorrow. I came to Frankfurt to take up a position with a noble family, but I lost my letter of introduction and they will not see me. To tell you the truth, your lordship, I am rather relieved; they seem to be rather arrogant – though this opinion might be born from my disappointment, I must concede."

"My dear young woman," said Ruprecht, "we would certainly have no trouble finding room for you in our coach for such a short journey, so long as my dear wife and my companions agree, but tell me, what position were you seeking?"

"Well, I have been a tutor for several young persons, teaching them the rudiments of reading, writing and figuring. My pupils have ranged from six to ten years. I have also acted as secretary and amanuensis to a noblewoman whose sight was failing her. I have letters of reference from some of my employers. As you might have gathered, I am without a position now and must find another soon, as I have no other means of support."

Euphemia spoke up at this point, "You are certainly welcome to join us tomorrow. We shall be setting out after breakfast – are you staying in this hotel?" "No, my lady, I merely came her for a meal this evening, spending my last few coins. I have been in Frankfurt only since this morning. I was brought here by a friend, who has since continued on his way, and he left before I found out that I had no position."

"In that case," said Euphemia, "you must be our guest tonight and take breakfast with us tomorrow. I am not merely being charitable, you should understand, I have an idea that we at the castle of Schloss Kirschbaum might have need of such an accomplished young woman as yourself. Here is my sister-in-law, the Landgravine Konstanze, who will catechize you further on this!"

The company moved into the sitting-room, and while the young woman was led to a couch by Konstanze, who engaged her in serious conversation, Ruprecht quietly asked Euphemia what this was all about, "What are you planning for this person? There are no children at the castle who need to be tutored – for a few years anyway – and neither you nor I have need of another secretary. Has Konstanze been talking to you about taking on another member of staff?"

Euphemia chuckled, "You are rather intrigued, are you not, dear brother? I am going to keep you in suspense a little longer – in good time, no doubt, Konstanze will make all of this clear to you."

As it happened, Konstanze was ready to do this almost as soon as she had finished talking with Fraulein Sonderhoff, whose hand she then took and brought her over to where Euphemia, Beatrice, Vincent and Ruprecht were sitting, saying, "I am delighted to announce that I have just engaged Angela Sonderhoff to be my amanuensis, editor and investigator, to work with me on a project that I have been planning and nurturing for a long time – even before I met Ruprecht and was courted and espoused by him."

"She has convinced me that she possesses the requisite skills in ample measure and has agreed to a trial period of six months, during which time both she and I will have the right to terminate the arrangement at a week's notice. But I see that an expression of puzzlement is growing on everyone's face save that of dear Euphemia, with whom I have been sharing my doubts and deliberations for several months. What, you are asking yourselves, is this mad woman blathering about?"

Her audience, of course, started to deny they had been having any such thoughts, but with a smile, Konstanze raised her hands to forestall this. "The simple answer," she said, "is that, with her help, I intend to write a history of the Landgravate of Hesse and of the family of Ruprecht of Henzel-Kirschbaum."

Chapter 25

The coach ride from Frankfurt to Schloss Kirschbaum started off being pleasant and uneventful. Once again they had provided themselves with picnic baskets, this time from the hotel kitchens, and luncheon was taken on a grassy meadow on a high bluff overlooking the river and was uninterrupted by intruders, save for pigeons looking for scraps. There was a fair amount of boat traffic to be seen on the river, including more than one sailing barge with red sails. As Vincent remarked, "It is impossible to confirm this from such a height, but I wonder whether Kapitän Kreutzer still plies the *Königen Emmeline* on this river – maybe he has embraced a comfortable retirement by now."

Said Wilfred, "I could fly down and see, if you wish!" but his offer was not taken up, Vincent saying, "We could enquire at the port office in Schloss Kirschbaum, but this is really not important, simply a little touch of nostalgia, which would be more so were Clotilda with us today."

Beatrice related, with much detail and elaboration, for the benefit of Konstanze and Angela, the story of the foiling of the silverware robbers, saying that it might well make an interesting interlude for their book, since it was an episode that had led to the foundation of Fritzi and Clotilda's business.

As they set off again, on each side of the road they saw broad fields of yellow flowers, which Vincent explained were called rapeseed or colza, "I know about this crop because it is one that interests beekeepers. Many farmers pay for hives to be placed in their fields so that the bees can help to pollinate the crop, improving seed production and the quantity of oil that they provide."

Said Beatrice, "That is very interesting! I never knew where colza oil came from. We live and learn, do we not?"

An hour or so later, Earnshaw, who was driving, rapped on the front window of the coach with the handle of his whip and called out, "There seems to have been an accident up ahead; it looks as though there is a poor horse tangled up with the harness of a wagon which has turned over in the ditch! When we get nearer, I will pull up and we can see if any help is needed."

Everybody piled out of the coach as it drew up, and then hastened to get back inside again as they saw swarms of angry bees buzzing about. They could see now that the wagon had been carrying a dozen bee-skeps, which were now scattered across the road, some upright and some overturned.

Vincent went toward the wagon and then raised both arms in the air and began a loud humming or buzzing. And then his companions beheld an amazing sight – the bees formed a swarm and approached him, some of them alighting for a while on his hands and arms. Soon the bees had all joined the swarm, which then moved off and settled on a branch of a tree growing in the hedgerow round the field.

Vincent said, with a sigh of relief, "At first I was not sure whether the bees here would behave in the same way as my own familiar creatures back home, but it seems that bees are bees! As you see, over the years, little by little, I have learnt how to commune with them. Now let us see to the wagon and the skeps – and where has the driver gone, I wonder?"

The others had ventured out of the coach now the bees were quieted, and Wilfred it was who found the driver, cowering in the ditch, some yards up the road. He persuaded him back to the wagon and Beatrice asked him whether he was injured.

"No, I don't think so, my lady," quavered the man, "but I feared for my life when the bees all flew at me! I'm not a beekeeper myself, I was just carrying them back from the fields for Master Steffanhaus, the keeper at Schloss Kirschbaum."

He helped Potter and Earnshaw to get his horse to its feet and calm it, and take it out of the harness, and then the drivers and the other men were able to right the wagon. The wagon driver explained that his horse had shied when an animal "Either a fox or a cat – I didn't get a good look at it!" had run across the road, and one wheel had dropped into the ditch, making the wagon overturn.

The skeps were retrieved and set back on the wagon, and then Vincent uttered another long buzzing sound, whereupon the bees, a few at a time, gradually made their way back into their hives. The wagon driver was mightily impressed by this performance, saying, "Not even Wilhelm Steffanhaus can do that, I'm sure, and he is a very good beekeeper!"

Beatrice asked him whether he had recovered fully and was prepared to continue, and the man said he was, thanking them all profusely for their help, and as the coach left, he raised his whip in salute while he coaxed his horse into motion.

Within the hour, the town and castle of Schloss Kirschbaum came into sight, and Ruprecht joined the drivers on the box and guided them through the streets and up to the stableyard. As they clattered in through the gateway, several grooms ran up to take the horses' heads and help the passengers down, and then the new chatelaine, Frau Hindenburg, came out to welcome them. Although as tall and stately, she seemed to be a much more sympathetic person than her predecessor, thought Vincent, who, like everyone else in the household, had always been slightly intimidated by Frau Angela Rosenmeyer.

Very soon, the party was settled in a sitting room and supplied with cool drinks and cakes, and many introductions were being made, most importantly to Konstanze's parents and her sister Filomena, who had been staying at the castle since the wedding. They explained that they had taken the opportunity of their daughter's marriage to refurbish and extend their own family home at Mittelheim; as Filomena explained, with a chuckle, "We have even added a new nursery against the possibility of visitations from the next generation!"

Tante Roswitha, walking a little stiffly with the aid of a stick, was entranced to meet Angela Sonderhoff, who she remembered as a little girl visiting the castle with her mother, when she was Roswitha's lady's maid. "So, will you be living here in the castle?" she asked, "Do you play an instrument? Please speak up, I am a little hard of hearing."

Euphemia went to the kitchen to discuss arrangements for dinner, causing several kitchen maids to be sent on errands to various shops – Mistress Zuber, the housekeeper, had fussed a little over the short notice, but Euphemia had no difficulty in soothing her, saying, "What we would like is good plain fare tonight – we have been eating in hotels, you know. But we shall certainly plan for a grand banquet or two over the next few weeks – we are still celebrating Beatrice's birthday!"

Later in the evening, all were settled in the grand dining-hall for dinner and there was no shortage of lively conversation. And then, the tables were cleared and the playing cards were brought out, together with nuts, raisins and liqueurs.

Chapter 26

Everyone was in agreement that a day or two of relaxation and quiet activities would be welcome after what had turned out to be a somewhat eventful journey from Woodhampton, so mostly they turned to domestic matters. Angela Sonderhoff was found a set of rooms not too far away from Konstanze's apartments, and given a sitting room equipped with a desk and plenty of bookshelves and cabinets for the documents she would need to accumulate while putting the history together.

Vincent sought out his beekeeper friend, Wilhelm Steffanhaus, to assure himself that the wagonload of bees had been delivered safely and then related his part in their recovery. Steffanhaus was duly impressed by this and pleaded to be acquainted with some of Vincent's skills. "I would only be too happy to pass them on directly if I could," said Vincent, "but I fear that there is no quicker way than by constantly observing the bees, studying their ways and practicing with them over a number of years, as I have done. Of course, while I am here, I will help you in whatever ways I can."

Beatrice and Euphemia lost no time in putting their heads together and consulting with Mistress Zuber about the forthcoming banquet, which they proposed to mount in a week or two. And they asked Konstanze whether they might borrow the services of Angela to help them in putting together a guest list, pointing out that this would familiarize her with family and friends and provide some useful background for the history.

Ruprecht spent a few hours in his office conferring with Herr Kraus, his secretary, and Herr Stringer, the bailiff of the estates, being brought up to date with the business affairs of the castle and its demesne. Most things had been proceeding quite smoothly in his absence, except that Robert Stringer reported that he had been forced to dismiss a pair of farmhands for selling estate produce at the market for their own profit. "I told them that I would take it no further with the constabulary this time, but that if I discovered that they were working on any local farm or estate, I would have no hesitation in informing the owner. This means, of course, that they will have to pack up and move out of the district, but I can have no sympathy for them, only for their families."

Ruprecht then told Friedrich Kraus about Lady Konstanze's history project, saying that he should feel free to disclose to her any information she requested. The secretary said that Herr Stringer was holding in his office a collection of daybooks, ledgers and journals for the castle that went back over a century, and that he would be only too pleased to explain them to Konstanze or to Fraulein Sonderhoff.

Then, Robert Stringer added, "Our bookkeeper, Giorgio Alessandro, who has been introducing to the estate the Genoese accounting system – which I myself do not yet understand fully, though I am struggling with it – will be instructed to do likewise."

For a while, only young Wilfred appeared to be at a loose end, until Tante Roswitha noticed him wandering aimlessly through the corridors and asked him whether he would do her a favour. Of course, he said he would, even before knowing what it might be, so she took him into her sitting room where her beloved spinet stood, surrounded by untidy piles of sheet music.

"As you may have noticed, but were too kind to mention, as well as being a little hard of hearing, I have to walk with the aid of a stick and cannot bend or stretch as I used to do. These ailments are the inevitable outcomes of my advancing age, I am afraid – but don't let me depress you, I have a good span of enjoyable years left to me, God willing."

"What I had in mind to ask you, dear Wilfred, is whether you might try to help me put my collection of music into order. Do you read and write well? Good, we shall see! And are you skilful with your hands in other ways – have you ever made pictures, for instance, by pasting leaves and flowers onto paper, or decorated the covers of your schoolbooks in like ways?"

Wilfred started to brighten up, his mind racing ahead in contemplation of what he might do, saying, "I suppose one way of dealing with all your piles of music would be to sort them into some order and then paste them into large ledger books or the like. Would that be the sort of thing you were thinking about, my lady?"

"I like the way you think, lad – but you will have to take your time over this, so as not to make mistakes you might regret later! But I want to mention the other side of the bargain – what it is that I should do for you in return. If you cannot already do

77

so, would you like to learn how to play the spinet? I believe I could be a good teacher, if you are prepared to work hard at this. I realize you will not be here in Schloss Kirschbaum for very long on this occasion, but when you return to Woodhampton, M. du Boise will be happy to take over as your music tutor, I would think."

"Yes, thank you very much, my lady, this is something that I have pondered on for some time. When I hear Lady Beatrice playing her marvelous new harpsichord I am filled with longing to do the same!" replied Wilfred. Roswitha could see that tears were welling up in his eyes, so she hugged him warmly, assuring him that she would have the better part of the bargain, "But when can you start on my untidy piles of papers, my boy? Would today be too soon?"

By dinnertime, everyone was ready to join in animated conversation, sharing with all the others what he or she had been engaged upon during the day.

And, at the end of the meal, Konstanze joined Roswitha and Wilfred in presenting a selection of ballads and madrigals, for both solo voice and combinations. Wilfred revealed that he was possessed of a soaring soprano, which blended with the ladies' voices to beautiful effect, and after some hesitation, Angela Sonderhoff was persuaded to join the ensemble as well.

But when Ruprecht stood up, ready to sing too, Euphemia clapped her hands and drew the musical interlude to an end, saying, "If you had ever heard Ruprecht's voice, as I have on numerous occasions over the years, you would realize that I have just done the company a huge favour!"

Ruprecht grimaced, but in good humour and said, "So, perhaps now is the time to play a few hands of cards – I find that I am acquiring rather a taste for that pursuit – but I see that some of us are already ready for bed. Before you all disperse, I would like to make an announcement. Since we have had a day of relaxation and recovery, I propose that we set out, tomorrow or the day after, for the family's hunting lodge in the mountains, which we can use as a base for enjoyable excursions of various kinds. The staff and some supplies have already been dispatched there to make the place ready to welcome us. Do we all agree to this proposal?"

There was general enthusiasm for this and conversation burst out again in small groups all around the hall.

Chapter 27

It was realized by the next morning that Ruprecht had not made a necessary allowance of time for the ladies to acquire suitable clothing for a country sojourn. Said Euphemia, "I suppose, my dear brother, that you simply intended to wear your own clothes from the last time we went to the mountains, at least two years ago! But I, for one, feel the need for at least two new sets of culottes – I assume we shall be riding when we are there – and those ladies, like Konstanze, who prefer to ride sidesaddle will need new habits, too. And that is to say nothing about dresses for day and evening wear! Men!"

So it was acknowledged that the excursion would have to be delayed a day or two. Angela timidly asked whether she would be allowed to go too, and was heartily assured that she was certainly thought of as more of a family member than a servant and that of course she might come. "Do you ride?" asked Konstanze, and Angela had to admit that she had not been on horseback since she was a young girl, but would welcome the opportunity to find out whether she still retained any of her skills.

The ladies were just about to set out for the shops in Schloss Kirschbaum when Fritzi and Clotilda arrived in Euphemia's sitting room, having dreamed themselves from Frankfurt, and so had to be told of the prospective holiday and invited to come too, if they could spare the time from their business.

"Of course we can!" said Fritzi, "All we need to do at our shop here in Schloss Kirschbaum town is to have a talk with the manager, Herr Lipschitz, and make sure that our business is proceeding well. We have always found him to be particularly efficient, so we anticipate that everything will have been running smoothly under his direction. We are very lucky to have his services, as well as those of Frau Gluck in Frankfurt, they are both very reliable managers."

Beatrice suggested that it would be pleasant if all were to make a day of it in the shops in town, "And we can have luncheon together while we are there in one or other of the smart restaurants – then we can peer at the other lady guests and make sure that the dresses we shall choose are up with the latest fashions!"

They all went down to the stableyard to ask for a carriage to be made ready for the short trip into town, and while Euphemia was speaking to Erik Leitner, the stable master, the Woodhampton drivers, Potter and Earnshaw, approached her with a question, "Excuse me, my lady, we have been told that there is a trip planned for the mountains shortly, but nobody on the staff here can tell us whether we two are to accompany you there," said Potter, "and we need to know if we are required to prepare our coach, or whether carriages from these stables will be used. In either case, we would like to beg that our Woodhampton steeds be granted a rest – they have worked well and hard and deserve a break for at least a few days."

Euphemia answered, somewhat shame-facedly, "You are quite right, Mr Potter, we should have taken you into our confidence. I will check with the Landgrave, whose brainchild this all is, and make sure you are informed at the earliest opportunity. And I promise to see to it that the brave Woodhampton horses are given a holiday in our demesne pasture – we have horses aplenty here at Schloss Kirschbaum to take us to the mountains."

The shopping expedition proved quite satisfactory, and Fritzi and Clotilda were reassured about the way their shop was being run, so on their return to the castle everyone set about packing their valises ready for departure early the next day. Beatrice had even bought some suitable clothing for Wilfred Pemberton, for which he was effusively grateful, since he had more or less only the clothes he had been wearing when they left Woodhampton. Beatrice said, "You had better change now and give your dirty clothes to the laundress, lest the animals we shall be hunting find it too easy to know when you are after them!"

Hearing this, Konstanze exclaimed, "I for one will not be wanting to take part in any hunting – I am not against hunting for meat or to control vermin, but I am rather uncomfortable about hunting for the sheer sport of it. I hope that this attitude is acceptable to the rest of the company, particularly to my dear husband!" And Clotilda and also Vincent, applauded this and said that they too would hope to find alternative recreations in the mountains.

Ruprecht embraced his wife and assured her that nobody, least of all himself, would think any the less of anyone who wished to abstain from that pursuit. Then Vincent asked whether there would be any opportunity for fishing in the mountain streams, as he had fond memories of joining his father in that occupation, years ago, and was told that he should talk to Fritzi, who was also fond of fishing and had little chance to indulge in it these days. On being approached, she clapped her hands and said, "What a good idea! I shall rummage through my cupboards and see whether I can still find my rods and other equipment! I can't remember the last time I had them out. I will certainly join you – as I recall, there are several likely streams not far from our lodge."

Over dinner there was much conversation about what everyone would do when they got to the lodge. As Vincent remarked, "We have all been assuming that the weather will stay fine – I do hope we shall not be disappointed!" to which Ruprecht commented that the autumn hereabouts could usually be relied on to be free of rain, although, of course, the days were beginning to become a little cooler. "But we have good fireplaces at the lodge, and plenty of firewood, so even were it to snow – which is unlikely at this season – we should all stay comfortable."

"Should we take rain clothes and warm coats?" asked Clotilda, "No need!" replied Euphemia, "there are coats and cloaks aplenty kept at the lodge against any eventuality."

As they prepared to leave the table, Ruprecht, who apparently saw himself as the director and organizer of the holiday, made a further announcement.

"We should set off good and early tomorrow – it is only a six-hour journey if we travel quickly, but we should allow plenty of time to admire the scenery as we go, especially those of us who are unfamiliar with the region, as there are scenes of great beauty to be enjoyed. If you look around this dining hall of ours, you will see depictions of many of the famed beauty spots in our land, and several of them you may be able to recognize as we travel up to the lodge. The former Landgrave, our father, was very interested in art and bought pictures from the artists. He also commissioned them to paint particular scenes, which you will see here or at the lodge. Of particular interest to those new to the castle is that large painting there, just to the left of the map of Hesse, upon which you can see the very hunting lodge of our destination – but I should point out that it was painted thirty years ago, and the lodge has been extended and rebuilt since a fire damaged it extensively soon afterwards."

Chapter 28

As Ruprecht had promised, the journey into the mountains and up to the lodge was a very pleasant one, interrupted only by interludes for sightseeing at notable vantage points, where could be seen wide vistas across the foothills to the high snow-capped ranges beyond, and by a rustic luncheon, plain but wholesome and delicious, taken in an establishment in the woods patronized mainly by timber-cutters. The party had certainly had their appetites stimulated by the cool mountain air, but in any case they found no cause to regard this meal with anything less than enthusiasm.

As was becoming a tradition with the company, they sang songs as they trotted along, accompanied by the flageolet of Earnshaw whenever he took a break from driving. The two carriages were under the control of the two Woodhampton drivers, Earnshaw and Potter and two of the Schloss Kirschbaum drivers, Schweissmann and Kohler. The two teams, as promised, were made up of Schloss Kirschbaum horses, including the two that had been confiscated by Vincent in France. The valiant horses from Woodhampton were taking their ease, Potter said, in a grassy paddock not far from the castle, and would be reinvigorated ready for the return trip, whenever it might be.

Arriving at the lodge, they were greeted cheerily by Frau Hindenburg and her small group of staff who had been sent ahead to prepare the way, and were shown to their quarters to unpack and prepare for dinner later in the evening. They gradually assembled in the main room of the lodge, whose most prominent feature was a central fireplace upon which a fire of logs blazed merrily.

Earnshaw was called upon again to entertain the assembly with his flageolet, and, the ice being broken, was soon joined by the ladies and Wilfred in a series of songs and ballads, some wistful, some happy. Ruprecht made one or two attempts to join in, but was prevented by Euphemia, who threatened him, only half humorously, with bodily force!

Vincent had never shown any inclination to burst into song, not even while travelling, but suddenly remembered that he had packed his flute and went to his room to fetch it, and soon he and Earnshaw were weaving complicated melodies in counterpoint to the delight of a hushed and rapt audience – Beatrice could be observed to be moving her fingers in concord on an invisible keyboard. By the time dinner was announced, the whole company had entered into a thoroughgoing holiday spirit.

The dinner was splendid, with as its centerpiece a whole roast boar, proudly presented by Herr Stringer, the resident huntsman, who was happy to see his efforts appreciated by the diners directly, instead of receiving messages of thanks at a few days' remove for the venison, hares and other game he dispatched from time to time to Schloss Kirschbaum.

After dinner, everyone adjourned to the main room again, where some played cards, some engaged in conversation about what they had seen on the journey as they sipped their drinks, and others were observed to be fighting the impulse to nod off – the trip and the mountain air had obviously had a relaxing effect.

Noticing this, Ruprecht rose to present suggestions for activities for the next day, "Of course, you are at liberty to do whatever you like – this is a holiday, not an organized programme – but you might like to form small groups, either to go fishing in the mountain streams and pools that I can tell you about, or to ride along the trails that the timber getters have made through the forest to drag out their logs, or simply to wander on foot through the woods. There are no real dangers from wild beasts in this area, but it would be as well to keep in pairs at the least, rather than setting off anywhere alone. Has anyone any questions of me at this point? If not, go and get a good night's sleep, everyone, wake refreshed and amuse yourselves!"

After breakfast everyone indeed chose different activities. Clotilda, Euphemia, Konstanze and Ruprecht selected steeds from the stable and set off along one of the forest trails; Fritzi and Vincent thought they might try the nearby streams for fish, and Beatrice, having found that there were canvases, brushes and paints stored at the lodge, took Wilfred with a supply of sketch-pads and charcoals to see whether they could find and capture a promising scene or two that could later be worked up into paintings.

As it happened, after a couple of hours, it was the latter pair who were the first to return to the lodge – Beatrice had started to feel ready for luncheon and Wilfred did not disagree, and they had made several sketches of scenes for painting. But as they approached the lodge, they were met at the steps by Frau Hindenberg, holding up her skirts at the sides so she could hurry, and with an anxious expression on her face.

"Oh, meine Dame, I am so relieved to see you – your mother is here, in considerable distress! I have settled her down in the small sitting room and given her a refreshing drink, but she would not tell me what was the trouble, only asking for you to be found quickly. I am so glad that you came along so soon – Lady Louise has only been here for perhaps half an hour since she magically appeared in the main room."

The housekeeper took Beatrice by the hand and led her into the lodge and to the sitting room, where they found Louise reclining on a couch, looking pale and with her eyes closed. As she heard Beatrice arrive, she opened her eyes and held out her arms to embrace her daughter. Frau Hindenberg withdrew, taking Wilfred with her, saying "Please ring if you need anything, meine Dame."

"Oh, Mama, whatever is the matter?" asked Beatrice, hugging and comforting her mother. Louise pulled herself together and said vehemently, but with tears filling her eyes, "It is your foolish brother, Brendan, once again, my dear – but this time he has really excelled himself – he is at present under the guard of the King's men in his apartment in the castle. I do not know what will become of him now – at the worst he will go to the gallows!"

"Why, what has he done?" asked Beatrice anxiously, imagining everything from traitorous plots to assault or even murder. "Well, it is not so much what he has done, but what he has refused to do!" said Louise, "I will now explain the situation to you briefly, my love. It all started, I gather, some weeks ago, when King Arnold, following the advice of his courtiers and of the nobility at large, resolved that it was his Christian duty to travel to the Holy Land, in support of crusaders from other countries, to recover the territory from the Saracens. So he realized that, there not being a standing army in England – we have fortunately not been in need of such a force for some years – he would have to approach his various barons and command them to raise detachments for this expedition. Well, to keep the story short, Brendan flatly refused to do this!"

Chapter 29

"Oh, Mama!" said Beatrice, hugging her mother and patting her back, as one comforts a hurt child, "Of course I will come back to Woodhampton with you without delay. Vincent's advice will be indispensible as well, and perhaps Ruprecht and even Euphemia could add their counsel? Who have you spoken to in England? I imagine there are those at Winchester whose experience would be priceless in such situations."

"Yes, of course!" replied Louise, "in particular, I have had long discussions with my dear old friend, Lord Hampshire, who still makes it his business to be conversant with court matters, even though he has been long retired from active participation in daily business. I myself have had much less to do at Winchester since your dear Papa passed away. And I have not yet been vouchsafed an appointment to talk to King Arnold personally, but I will certainly do that if he will receive me."

Beatrice was puzzled, "Was it not the King who decreed that Brendan be arrested, then?" "No, no!" said her mother, "The general who was delegated to select those who would be required to supply troops was Lord Hoxteth, from the North, I believe. I saw him but briefly and he struck me as a man with a rather rigid approach to affairs – a typical military man!"

As they were talking, they became aware of voices and movement in the main room. Beatrice excused herself and left the sitting room, wanting to warn whoever was out there that her Mama was in a distressed state. She found that they were Vincent and Fritzi, who had just returned from their fishing excursion. Before she could speak, Vincent asked her in urgent tones, "Have you seen Fraulein Sonderhoff this morning? Nobody seems to know where she might be, and I am concerned lest she went walking in the woods by herself and has become lost!"

"Vincent, that is indeed a worry!" said Beatrice, "But I must tell you that I am at present trying to come to terms with a greater one – could you please leave the task of looking for Angela to Fritzi, if she wouldn't mind, and come with me to speak to my Mama, who has come here to us for help of a more serious and pressing nature!"

When Vincent saw how upset Louise was looking, he immediately embraced her and gently asked her to tell him what it was all about. Having heard her account, he became very serious, saying, "As soon as Ruprecht and the others return from their ride, we shall plan what we should do. Of course, this will inevitably involve some or all of us dreaming ourselves to Woodhampton, but we should not just take action precipitately without discussing what options are open to us – and to do this we need to find out much more about what the King and his advisors have in mind."

Then Beatrice spoke up again, "Mama, please be assured that we shall all do what we can to rescue this unfortunate boy – I say boy because he is still a callow youth inside, even though he is nearly thirty years old! Nevertheless, he is still accountable for his actions – I surmise that his immaturity will not be regarded as an excuse by those who are accusing him."

"Now, dear Mama, while we await the return of the others from their ride, you need to take some nourishment – how long has it been since you ate last?"

"You are right, of course, my darling Beatrice – at times like this I find I can easily forget to look after myself properly. Let us see whether we can be provided with luncheon right away. I must say that I am impressed with this place! When I heard 'hunting lodge' mentioned, I confess I pictured some sort of cabin in the wilderness!"

Beatrice smiled and said, "That reminds me to ask whether you found the lodge easily as you dream travelled?"

"Well, of course, I dreamt myself to Schloss Kirschbaum first, and then asked Tante Roswitha and the staff. I was shown the painting of the old hunting lodge and was assured that the new-built one had a sufficient number of familiar features about it that I would have no difficulty in recognizing it. I was then shown the map of Hesse and had the road I should follow pointed out. The rest was rather straightforward! In fact, I saw a mounted group on a track not far from the lodge, who might have been your companions, but I was intent on reaching here and did not consider approaching them. In any case they could have been strangers, I did not fly very low to inspect them closely."

The topic of Brendan's predicament was avoided over luncheon, and a pleasant meal and conversation were enjoyed by all. Just as they were thinking of leaving the table, a clatter was heard outside, presaging the entry of the riding party into the dining room. They had obviously had an energetic and agreeable morning, and started to tell Beatrice and Vincent all about it when they suddenly realized that Lady Louise was there in the room. As Euphemia said, "What a nice surprise to see that Louise has decided to join us here for a holiday!" to which Louise sadly replied, "Oh were it as simple as that!"

Questions and explanations followed and the mood became rather more sober. After some deliberation, it was agreed by all that they would stay at the lodge for dinner, then have a good night's sleep (as Beatrice remarked, Louise seemed to be in great need of rest) and then Beatrice, Vincent and Ruprecht would dream travel with Louise back to Woodhampton the next morning.

Ruprecht pointed out to the others that it was their decision whether or not to stay at the lodge or to return to Schloss Kirschbaum – they would be welcome either way.

But, before doing anything further, there was still the matter of Angela Sonderhoff – as far as anyone knew, Fritzi was still looking for her! At last, someone thought to ask Frau Hindenburg, who said, with no hesitation, "I'm sorry, I knew not that you were unaware of what Fraulein Sonderhoff has been doing all day. She is down with Herr Stringer, the huntsman, in his office next the stables, looking through the records and accounts of the lodge since it was first built. She was telling us that Lady Konstanze is to write a history, and that she is helping her. I believe that Countess Friederike is also down there with them now."

Those two studious ladies were soon rounded up, and everyone repaired to the dining room for the usual sumptuous lodge dinner. Louise was persuaded to take a little wine, and she was soon able to set aside her worries for a while and join in the jesting and conversation.

Nobody was late for breakfast the next day, and the travelling party gathered in the small sitting room where Louise started the humming. Before long they were swooping high over the countryside, following a route that Ruprecht now knew like the back of his hand. As they arrived in the main sitting room of the castle, they found Mr Pemberton waiting for them, looking important and ready to make an announcement.

Chapter 30

The Majordomo bowed to Louise and acknowledged the others with a gesture. "Only an hour or so since, my Lady, a Royal courier arrived from Winchester on horseback, accompanied by his squire. When I told him that I expected you shortly, he was disposed to wait for you before delivering his message from King Arnold, which he said was highly confidential. I have put the pair in the small dining room and ordered that they be provided with suitable refreshments."

"Thank you, Mr Pemberton," said Louise, "Lady Beatrice and I will receive him in my sitting room in a little while – I will tell you when. Please see to it that we are brought some light refreshments there, and ask my friends what they would like. Please, everyone, do not approach these messengers before they are summoned to my apartment."

Vincent and Ruprecht remained in the main sitting room, telling the maid that they would not take any refreshments at that time. Before Mr Pemberton left Ruprecht enquired of him about Brendan's situation. "Oh, sir, Lord Musgrave is still confined to his apartment, guarded by two of the King's soldiers at all times. There are six of them in the castle now, together with a Captain Ferris, who is their commander. They allow food and drink to be brought to him, but they check the tray and dishes scrupulously every time. He complained of boredom, and since then Captain Ferris has been going into his apartment from time to time and playing a few hands of cards – piquet mostly, I believe. He also has books in his apartment, of course, but I have never known him to be a great reader. Now I must go and see when Lady Louise will be ready to receive the courier."

Vincent and Ruprecht began to speculate over the situation. Said Vincent, "I am a little encouraged by the fact that Brendan has not as yet been taken away to Winchester or London. This makes me think that he is not being treated as a traitor, but perhaps being given the chance to reconsider his refusal."

"I am not familiar with the English law," said Ruprecht, "but I have assumed that King Arnold has every right as sovereign to demand of his barons that they provide him with men and whatever else he should desire of them – horses, ships, munitions and every other type of supply. Is the penalty for refusal laid down in any statute, do you know? And over what men does a baron hold sway?"

"As to the last," replied Vincent, "my understanding is that a baron's fiefdom extends to those he employs for wages or for kind and also to those who are the tenants of his lands, which are in any case held only at the pleasure of the King."

At this point, there came a knock on the door and they were approached by a footman, saying that Lady Louise had requested their presence in her apartment, where the royal courier was about to present her with the King's proclamation. Arriving at her door, they were shown into Louise's sitting room by Mr Pemberton, who then withdrew.

It was clear that Lady Louise was in command of the situation and was sitting, straight-backed, next to Beatrice on a settee, while the courier and his attendant stood before her, shuffling a little.

"Landgrave Ruprecht and Mr Crabbe," Louise said, "I would like to introduce to you the King's Messenger, Sir Lionel Fitz-Harris, who will convey His Majesty's decisions to us. Please be seated, gentlemen. Now, Sir Lionel, if you would be so kind – the King's words."

It was clear from the courier's demeanour that he was accustomed to be in a more commanding position than he was at the moment. Nevertheless, he cleared his throat, unrolled a parchment, and spoke.

"Here are the commands of His Majesty King Arnold, by the Grace of God, Sovereign of this land of England and commander of all its forces."

"Inasmuch as Brendan, Baron Musgrave, has declined to acquiesce to His Majesty's lawful demand for military personnel and supporting resources, the following edict is proclaimed."

"If after the elapse of thirty days from the day of the original demand, the Baron Musgrave still refuses to comply, then the castle and demesne of Woodhampton, with all its appurtenances, will be seized by the King, and Baron Musgrave will be banished from this kingdom. The King, in his mercy, and taking account of the services to the crown formerly given by the Baron's family, and especially by Lady Louise de

Gonville Musgrave, including the defeat of those traitors who would have usurped the throne, will not exact any punishment beyond the banishment. And that banishment extends only to the person of Brendan, Baron Musgrave. His family and their entire entourage are welcome to continue to occupy those parts of the castle not required by King Arnold and the royal family and staff. God Save the King!"

The courier bowed, rolled up the parchment, and added, "The King desired me to add the following remarks, which he enjoins you not to publish abroad. He has been advised that, were he to follow his personal desires and not to exact any punishment at all, that this would dangerously weaken his authority over the nobility and country at large."

"I am further commanded to instruct the captain of the detachment who is at present guarding Baron Musgrave to release him to his family forthwith. He will be allowed to make what arrangements he thinks fit to leave this country within the space of sixty days further. While he is required to satisfy the King's representatives that he is complying honourably with the edict, he is not to be regarded or treated as a felon."

Lady Louise stood and offered her hand to Sir Lionel, who kissed it. "Now," she said, "that you have executed your somewhat distasteful task dutifully, you must join us in the small dining room for luncheon before you take horse again for Winchester."

It was a very quiet Brendan who joined them shortly thereafter, to be embraced warmly by his sister, rather more so by his mother, who was somewhat tearful, and greeted cordially by Vincent and Ruprecht.

They all proceeded to the dining room and managed to throw off their immediate sombre thoughts. But the question in everyone's mind was soon articulated by Beatrice. "Where will you go, Brendan, and what is to become of your fiancée?"

"Well, my dear Florence has said she will stand by me, so she and I are still engaged and intend to marry in a few months, as previously agreed. With her parents' permission, and if Lady Hermione Bagshott is willing to continue being our chaperone, we shall ask Ruprecht, Konstanze and Euphemia whether they are willing to tolerate me and become our hosts. If so, we shall take up residence at Schloss Kirschbaum, under similar conditions to those that were arranged for Woodhampton."

Chapter 31

When luncheon and conversation were at an end, Sir Lionel, the courier, rose and said, "My lords, ladies and gentlemen, I must now make my farewells and return with my aide to Winchester. But I have one further duty to perform. Her Majesty, Queen Tabitha, entrusted me with a personal letter that I was to deliver to Lady Louise only when it was clear that matters here were safely in train towards a satisfactory settlement. My lady, please accept this with my own good wishes."

Louise accepted the rolled and sealed document, offering her hand for the messenger to kiss. Once he and his squire had left, the atmosphere in the room became suddenly more relaxed and general chatter broke out. Louise went to her son, hugged him warmly again and then withdrew to take her seat on a couch at the side of the room, where she unsealed and unrolled the letter. She read it through twice and then raised her hand for attention.

"This is good news, of interest to everyone here," she announced, "It starts with warm greetings from Queen Tabitha and King Arnold, and then goes on to explain that the royal couple thought it best to maintain a certain reserve until it was certain that Brendan had accepted the King's edict. But, that being resolved, and in the knowledge that the seizure of our castle would inevitably cause a certain awkwardness, Queen Tabitha goes on to declare her desire to maintain close and friendly relationships with us all, adding that King Arnold is of a like mind. So, to cut things short, she proposes that she and the King come here on a lengthy visit, starting in three days' time, to become properly acquainted!"

Beatrice asked whether Queen Tabitha had made any mention of plans for changing around the accommodation at the castle to accord with its new owners, but Louise replied, "She certainly did not – that would have been premature, even impolite, wouldn't you think? In any case, Florence and Brendan should not be given the feeling that they are being hounded out of the castle!"

"No, Mama, you are right!" said Beatrice, "But perhaps we should start to think about it, nevertheless. Will the royal couple need any more than Brendan's, Florence's and

Hermione's apartments, which will all soon become vacant? Oh, I suppose they will be bringing hordes of staff as well – valets, equerries, ladies-in-waiting, maids and so forth. Ah well, maybe we had better wait until they come, after all!"

So it was decided that, since there were more pressing decisions to be made before then, questions of accommodation should be deferred for the moment.

Ruprecht took up Brendan's request that he and Florence be allowed to move to Schloss Kirschbaum castle, "We will certainly make you welcome there, and Lady Hermione, too. And, I venture that Konstanze and Euphemia are looking forward with great pleasure to helping with the arrangements for your wedding! Not so long ago, Euphemia took a prominent part in Konstanze's and my own nuptials, in the role of Brautjungfer – do you say 'maid of honour'?"

The next few days passed very swiftly – even though the King and Queen were not yet taking up permanent residence, they still had to have a guest suite prepared for them. Fortunately, the castle was amply provided with guest accommodation – it had not even been fully used up for all the guests who came to Beatrice's birthday celebrations – and so the same apartments that the royal couple had occupied then were specially polished up and tidied. And there was much consultation between Louise, Beatrice and Mistress Travis the housekeeper about planning the menus for the royal stay.

And on the appointed day, a procession of two carriages and half a dozen mounted soldiers swept into the forecourt of Woodhampton Castle, bringing the royal couple and their immediate staff, and a number of palace officials, military officers and servants.

King Arnold kissed the hands of Louise and Beatrice and shook hands with Ruprecht and Vincent – Brendan had thought it best to absent himself from the welcome – and Queen Tabitha first embraced Louise warmly, unable to hold back a few tears, saying that she hoped that the unfortunate circumstances that had brought them all together on this occasion could soon be swept away and forgotten. Then she took Beatrice by the hand as they walked into the main hall of the castle, saying, "We have so much to talk about! I shall love living here with you when we move in permanently – we shall be just like sisters! I'm afraid that my relations with own sister, Margarethe, have been rather strained over the last few years. I believe she may have taken offence because I, the younger sister, met and married my dear Prince Arnold, before she had a chance to find a husband of her own, and she felt rather left out. I'm afraid that she has somewhat withdrawn from the world and retreated to her mansion in York. I do see her from time to time, but it is never the same as when we were young."

After dinner that first evening, Louise drew Vincent aside and said, "I have been wondering whether we might invite our other friends and relations at Schloss Kirschbaum to come and join us while the royal couple are visiting, particularly Konstanze, of course, but also Fritzi, Roswitha, Clotilda and Angela Sonderhoff. I did remember to dream myself there, after the courier's visit, to confide in Konstanze about her future guests and confirm she was in agreement, so they have a general notion that all is proceeding reasonably well here, but they really deserve a chance to meet the King and Queen once again – of course, Roswitha and Angela have never even been here!"

Vincent agreed heartily, and undertook to go and fetch them all by dream travel, but wondered whether it might not be courteous to ask the King and Queen whether they were agreeable, first of all.

Louise said, "As usual, sensible Vincent knows what is right and proper! I believe they might be ready to speak of this now, I will send to find out." A footman was dispatched with this message, and he soon returned to say that the King and Queen would be happy to receive them in their apartment.

Tabitha and Arnold greeted Louise and Vincent warmly, and after some inconsequential chat had no hesitation in saying they were ready to welcome new guests.

And then Louise thought of something further. "Your Majesty," she said to the King, "I have already bestowed the gift of tongues on her Majesty the Queen – I believe that you might also find it valuable, particularly as we are soon to be overwhelmed by a group of German speakers. Would you permit me to give this gift to you?"

"Of course, my dear Louise – I shall be honoured! Even though I still remember my Danish, facility in all tongues would be very welcome." And very soon it was done, and the King amused himself by conversing in Finnish with Vincent.

Chapter 32

As promised, the next day Vincent dream-travelled to Schloss Kirschbaum and brought back the others, but also passed on a message from Frauen Hindenburg and Zuber, the chatelaine and the housekeeper of the castle, who wished to enquire whether the banquets that they had been planning were now to be cancelled.

"But of course not!" exclaimed Euphemia, "They have merely been postponed a little – how could we think of abandoning such an important part of Beatrice's birthday revels! I will send word, or dream-travel there myself, to reassure them of our intentions."

While Roswitha and Angela were being introduced to the King and Queen – Fritzi and Clotilda, of course, were already well-established friends – Louise and Euphemia asked whether Tabitha and Arnold would like to visit Schloss Kirschbaum to continue the birthday celebrations.

"I am afraid that we shall have to decline your kind invitation," said King Arnold regretfully, "Protocol demands that a reigning monarch not visit a foreign country without the full panoply of a state visit, accompanied by diplomats and other high personages. We could, of course, visit secretly, under assumed names, but I am disinclined to take such a risky course this early in my reign – besides I am committed to leave for the Holy Land before the end of the year at the head of my companies of crusaders, who are at this very season being assembled and trained. No, no, let us, if we may, simply enjoy a few days as your guests here at Woodhampton."

Queen Tabitha added, "And please let Brendan know that we are happy to meet with him at a social level – he is bound to feel awkward – as I must confess so do Arnold and I – but his banishment is an affair of state that has already been promulgated to the world at large and has nothing personal about it."

"That is extremely generous of you, your Majesties!" said Louise, "I think it will do the young man some good to realize these things! I believe that, at last, some degree of maturity is taking hold of him – the attempt at elopement was a beginning for this."

"But now," exclaimed Beatrice, "We must decide what shall be our activities over the next few days while our royal guests are with us here. I would hazard the thought that some light-hearted diversions would be welcome after the dramatic events that we have all been through!"

"Mayhap our royal guests have some preferences," suggested Vincent, "or we can offer them a few options based on what we between us have found entertaining recently, both here and in Hesse. I could name a few activities immediately myself, let us see – riding, fishing, dancing, card-playing, musical performances, talking, walking in the woods and fields, and so on and so on. What do you say, your Majesties?"

King Arnold laughed out loud, "Why, whatever is the most distant from affairs of state, political intrigue and mischief-making! I am just beginning to realize how tense all these matters have made me in recent months. How about you, Tabitha, my dear?"

"Well, you may think my request rather unusual, mayhap even strange, but I would like to take the opportunity offered by this break from my busy round of social engagements to search, in a leisurely way, for a new companion!" replied the Queen, "No, Arnold, I am not becoming tired of thee! What I speak of is not another human friend, but a dog!"

Beatrice laughed in pleasure, "Oh, Tabitha, I think I know what you mean! We in this household have enjoyed the company of such faithful beasts for long years – at the moment you may have seen that, once again, we have a beagle here in the castle. But perhaps you have in mind a dear little fluffy white creature that you can carry in your muff?"

"Oh, no, no!" said Tabitha, "I have often seen ladies at court spoiling such little pets with tidbits from their plates, so that they become fat and spiteful. No, what I want is a dog who will accompany me on walks in the park and fetch sticks that I throw, an energetic dog of decent size! Does anyone here know of a likely place that I might see some dogs from which to choose? I have no idea how one goes about such a quest – are there dealers in dogs, as there are in horses and cattle?"

"There certainly are!" declared Vincent, "We could ask our deputy stable-master, Clive, about this, since Mr Potter is still in Schloss Kirschbaum, or else we could talk to old Luke Sampson, the chief shepherd and flock-master of the estate.

Both of those gentleman circulate in the livestock markets of the town, and if they don't know themselves, they will know who to ask."

The Queen was very pleased to hear this, "So can we start looking this afternoon?" she asked, "As you can readily tell, I am very keen to set off on this venture."

"Very well, your Majesty," responded Vincent, "As soon as you desire, I will take you down to the stables and we will find out where Sampson might be today."

In less than two hours, Vincent and Tabitha were trotting along in the chaise, heading for a farmhouse where they had been told they could find James Thurston, a breeder of foxhounds, who also dealt with other kinds of dog. Mr Clive had given as his opinion that a foxhound was not what the Queen wanted, as they worked best in packs. "See what Mr Thurston suggests," he said, "I have always found him very knowledgeable and helpful."

When they arrived at the farm, a boy offered to fetch Thurston, who appeared from a long shed, from which could be heard the sounds of barking and baying – it was evidently feeding time.

When he found that it was the Queen who wanted to make enquiries, Thurston was a little overwhelmed, and even started to stammer as he answered her questions, until Tabitha told him she was merely a customer today, and off-duty from being a Queen. She explained what sort of dog she had in mind, in general terms, and he thought for a moment and then lifted a finger.

"Come with me, your Majesty and sir, I will show you some puppies who are now just old enough to be taken from their mother."

Tabitha and Vincent were taken into a large shed, divided into pens containing mainly foxhounds, but, in the corner, was a pen with a large black dog and two little black puppies. "These are what are called retrievers," said Thurston, "they can be used as hunting dogs, to retrieve game, as their name suggests, but they have a wonderful nature and make faithful family pets. When your Majesty has children, begging your pardon for my presumption, you will find that they get on well with them."

"Wonderful," said Tabitha, "I'll take them both!"

Chapter 33

When the Queen and Vincent arrived back at the castle, carrying a puppy each to the sitting room, the word soon got around and people clustered around the new arrivals, picking them up for hugs and telling them how beautiful they were and so on. Beatrice asked Tabitha what their names were.

"They have been given none as yet," was her reply, "but I was thinking about that in the chaise on the way here. They are both males, and I would like to give them names that will suggest noble qualities. What think you, Beatrice, of 'Joris' and 'Hero'? The meaning of 'Hero' is clear, and I like the name 'Joris' because my favourite uncle in Denmark, who I admired greatly when I was small, bore that name."

"They sound like excellent choices, dear Tabitha, but which puppy is which – I cannot tell them apart! But wait, this one has a little nick in his ear – perhaps he has been squabbling with his brother!"

"Well, then, he shall be 'Hero', since he seems to be otherwise unscathed!" said Tabitha, picking him up, caressing him and murmuring, "Good Hero, nice Hero, what a good boy!" and other inconsequential sayings. She also made sure to pet the other one, Joris, to the same degree.

Lady Louise had been watching all this fussing with some amusement, but then became more serious, "Your Majesty, when you have a moment, please bring your two new friends to my apartment, where I will present them and you with a special gift." She then excused herself to the rest of the company and left the room.

All the excitement had proved to be a little too much for Hero, who went into a corner and left a puddle. Said Vincent, "Well, we cannot blame the little fellow, but this demonstrates that we shall have to take steps to house-train them (or castle-train them!), lest they become very unpopular with the house staff! Wilfred, are you willing to undertake this duty? I hardly think that it would be meet for her Majesty to do this!" Wilfred said he would be only too happy, "And I shall take them for walks also, when Queen Tabitha is too busy!"

At this point, Tabitha asked Wilfred to carry Hero, while she picked up Joris, and they took the two puppies to Louise's apartment, where they found her attending to some accounts.

"I am afraid that I shall have to take over the castle business from Brendan once again – but your Majesty should not feel any sense of guilt over this – to tell the truth I have been quietly checking on my son's work for some time, since he has not the right character for meticulous figuring! But, please, Tabitha, come and sit on this couch, with a dog on either side. Thank you for your help, Wilfred, you may go now."

Louise drew up a chair facing the couch and explained, "I am deeply sensible of the merciful approach that King Arnold has taken over the business with Brendan. I do not have to tell you, Tabitha, that he had it in his power to exact a much more terrible penalty. I would have liked to express my appreciation to him directly, but I felt that this would be improper, so I resolved to do it in a roundabout way. And these sweet dogs have given me an opportunity."

"As you are aware, I am what is called a wise woman. You have seen that I am able to confer magical gifts on whomsoever I think worthy, but my powers do not stop there. I have the ability to heal many ailments and injuries, and I can perform enchantments. As a so-called 'white witch' I am not permitted, or indeed able, to enchant human beings, but I can work these magic spells on animals – and that is what I propose to do now, with your two new dogs."

"We are all well aware that the normal lifespan for a dog is hardly more then a score of years, sometimes much less, which means that we often have the sad task of saying farewell to creatures that have become fast friends and loyal companions. I can help here! What I am able to do is to endow these two, Hero and Joris, with a lifespan that will closely match that of their mistress – you, your Majesty. Would you like me to do this, Tabitha?"

"Oh, yes, Louise, please do! I have several times had the sad experience you have mentioned, with pet dogs and cats. In a private place at my old home in Denmark there is a small graveyard devoted to family pets – not only mine, but those of my sister, Margarethe."

Lady Louise nodded happily, "So I will do this service for you, my dear. And I shall also make sure that they grow up big, strong and healthy. You may some time in the future need their aid in trying circumstances – this is impossible to predict, I may be a wise woman, but I am not a seer!"

"And before I start the enchantment, I would like to point out something that not everyone who has the gift of tongues realizes – animals have their own language, too, so anyone with that gift can converse with animals as well. Like any human youngsters, your puppies will not yet have developed their own language fully, but you and they can practice together. Believe me, this ability is of great help in training animals!"

Louise asked Tabitha to rest her hands on the puppies' heads, to calm them. They were already becoming fond of her, it seemed. The Louise knelt in front of the couch and intoned a series of words or sounds. Not even with her gift of tongues could Tabitha follow what was said, but the two little dogs soon closed their eyes and let out great sighs.

"It is done!" said Louise with a smile, kissing Tabitha on both cheeks, "You don't know these little creatures, so you will not notice any changes in their behaviour immediately, but in time you will find they are more faithful and intelligent that any pet you may have had in the past."

Louise and Tabitha went to join the others in the large sitting room, and Hero and Yoris trotted after them as though tied to the Queen with strings. Louise whispered in Tabitha's ear, whereupon she clicked her tongue and pointed to a place by the wall. The two dogs ran there and lay down side by side, regarding their mistress keenly for her next instructions.

Everyone clapped, and Tabitha explained what had just been happening, saying, "Dear Louise has just given me a precious gift, and I shall now be able to cherish my dogs all my life. Thank you again, Louise, I bless the day that I first met you and your family – not excluding poor Brendan."

As they all went in to dinner that evening, much of the conversation concerned pets and working animals, and the ways that human beings and their humble allies could live and work together.

After the meal, Wilfred proudly took Hero and Joris for a final walk, before settling them into their special place in the stables.

And Queen Tabitha could have been observed to slip down there to bid them goodnight!

Chapter 34

As had been promised, the guests and residents took up Beatrice's invitation and Vincent's suggestions to freely engage in a number of recreational pursuits over the next few days, some indoors or in the grounds of the castle, others in the town and the surrounding countryside.

Tante Roswitha was greatly impressed by Beatrice's new harpsichord, and sat on its bench admiring its decorations wistfully until Beatrice exhorted her not to be shy, but to feel free to play it, whereupon she set to with a delighted smile on her face. She confined herself to the principal keyboard for a while, but eventually dared to essay playing on both manuals and experimenting with the different registers they could produce.

"You will have to come and drag me to the table at mealtimes!" she exclaimed, "Or else my skeletal remains will ultimately be discovered here, with my bony fingers still striking chords!"

And Tante Fritzi, when she was not out riding with Beatrice, Euphemia and Konstanze, indulged in her newly-awakened passion for fishing, having been shown a stream near the demesne that was full of more than a few varieties of fish. Mistress Travis was happy to accept her catch, and made sure that her best cook was given free rein to produce delicious different ways to serve the fish to a few select diners – unfortunately there was never quite enough to go round everyone. As Fritzi said, "I fish for enjoyment, not out of necessity!"

As for Queen Tabitha and King Arnold, they seized the opportunity of being away from the Winchester court to enjoy simple relaxed pleasures, like walking through the woods with Joris and Hero – accompanied at a discreet distance by two men of the royal guard – or just sitting on the terrace in the sun during the afternoons while it was still warm, chatting with anyone who cared to join them.

Behind these tranquil scenes there were two enterprises being quietly planned. The first of these was a grand ball and banquet to which would be invited many friends and relations, many of them those who had previously attended Beatrice's birthday party. The arrangements were being made by Louise and

Mistress Travis, while Florence had been invited to take part, because, as Louise said, "She will have to get used to being a hostess some time, particularly when she and Brendan set up their own establishment – they will not be able to stay at Schloss Kirschbaum indefinitely!"

And then the alterations that would have to be made to the castle in preparation for Brendan's departure and the official arrival of the King and Queen and their staff were also being discussed seriously by a group comprised of Louise, Beatrice, Vincent, Mr Pemberton and the builder, Mr Hutchinson.

At one of the first of their meetings, Louise had also suggested that Lord Hampshire be asked for his opinion, as he would be able to recall the time when the late King, Adelbert, was on the throne, and so would have a thorough understanding of what might be needed for the new royal couple and their extensive staff, as it was becoming clear from what had been said in conversations that King Arnold and Queen Tabitha intended in future to spend more of their time at Woodhampton than at Winchester.

"We shall, of course," said Louise, "when major decisions need to be made, consult the King and Queen in detail, but we must not bother them too soon, since they are supposed to be on holiday from matters of state. But I have gained the distinct impression from Queen Tabitha that she and the King want to avoid Woodhampton becoming the social hub of the kingdom that Winchester Castle was and still remains, swarming with idlers and a centre for intrigue."

With each successive meeting, Mr Hutchinson, who took a practical, down-to-earth approach to his work, would spread out the latest version of his plans, at first mere sketches, but as time went on, more and more detailed and precise. As he pointed out, a lot could be achieved by alterations and the reassignment of rooms, but that there was a need for extensions to be built to some of the upper floors, since the royal apartments would best be situated on the top levels of the castle. This, fortunately, could be achieved by enclosing some of the existing rooftop terraces.

Some of the work could be put in train as soon as Brendan, Florence and the Countess Hermione took themselves to Schloss Kirschbaum, but most of the serious rebuilding would be best done when there were no longer guests in residence.

Angela Sonderhoff proved to be a serious student and researcher – as well as joining in some of the recreational pursuits with the others, she undertook to delve into the records of Winchester Castle to discover what was written there about the diplomatic activities at court of the former Landgrave, judging this to be an aspect of his life and career which would form an essential chapter of Konstanze's history of the Landgravate of Hesse. She also took the opportunity to talk to Lord Hampshire about these matters on one of his visits to Woodhampton.

Brendan was seemingly making a great deal of effort to take his departure from Woodhampton and, indeed, England, in as graceful a way as possible. He had taken to confiding often in Vincent, as well as in Beatrice, while he was still rather intimidated by his Mama, Lady Louise and therefore acted in a reserved manner with her.

One morning he sought Vincent's advice about what items might be considered proper to take with him from the castle to Schloss Kirschbaum when he should depart with Florence and Hermione.

"I have no difficulty in thinking about my personal effects," he said, "what I am wondering about are such things as furniture and carriages. Florence will take her clavichord of course – that is hers personally – but should we take our desks and our cupboards? And we shall need a carriage or two when we are in Hesse – we can't keep borrowing from Ruprecht and Konstanze, can we?"

Vincent had an idea about the carriage. "We took the big coach from Woodhampton on our last voyage, of course. It is still in Schloss Kirschbaum, and it would seem foolish to bring it back to England by ship and then take another over for you. Why don't we arrange for Potter and Earnshaw to drive it back to Boulogne to meet you when the time comes, and then that can become your own. And when you decide how much of a heavy nature you wish to take with you, we can similarly arrange for a cart or carts from Schloss Kirschbaum to meet the ship and convey it onward."

Brendan was very taken with this plan, saying, "I can always rely on you for sensible suggestions, Vincent. You wouldn't like to become my personal advisor, would you? No – I suppose not – you are too strongly attached to my Mama and to Beatrice!"

Chapter 35

After Brendan had left, Vincent found himself thinking about what he had said, "– you are too strongly attached to my Mama and to Beatrice!" and wondered just what he meant. Certainly, Vincent and Beatrice had been firm friends since childhood and had shared in many adventures, but surely there was no suggestion of any more intimate bond than that? He would have to talk with Beatrice and discover her thoughts on the subject.

Meanwhile, there was business to be done, and tonight was the occasion of the grand banquet and ball. The guests started arriving in the early afternoon, and Louise, Beatrice and Vincent, took turns in welcoming them and getting the staff to take them to their accommodation to change and make themselves ready.

Beatrice had taken it upon herself to send an invitation to Lady Margarethe, Queen Tabitha's sister, at her residence in York, and was gratified when she arrived, greeted Beatrice and Louise cordially, and asked whether her sister was in residence. Anyone who observed the subsequent meeting of the two would have had no inkling of any coolness or distance between them, and Beatrice gave an inward sigh of relief.

When Florence's parents, the Duke and Duchess of Dorset, arrived they were still in need of reassurance about the difficulty of the situation, but the signs of strain on their faces were soon removed when they met Brendan and found that he was fully reconciled to his banishment, and was even cheerfully making plans for how he and Florence would cope with removing to their new abode at Schloss Kirschbaum.

As Beatrice said, "Nothing has ever gone very deep with my dear brother, but I have never thought him as badly intentioned, merely superficial. But from what I have gathered of Florence, she has strength enough to act as a steadying influence for him, young though she might be. Let us fervently hope so, anyway!"

But as she and the Duke and Duchess and the other guests were seated ready in the dining hall, awaiting the entry of the King and Queen, a footman came and spoke quietly to Lady Louise, who then got to her feet with a gesture of annoyance, beckoned

Beatrice to follow her, and swept out into the hallway. Outside the hall they saw waiting the by now familiar figure of Sir Lionel Fitz-Harris, the royal courier. He had been bringing routine dispatches from Winchester for the King about every two days, but this time he looked rather more grim than usual.

Said Lady Louise, "What is afoot, Sir Lionel? The King and Queen will be arriving at our banquet soon, I do hope that your news is nothing that will upset our festivities!"

"I certainly share your sentiments, my lady. Until I have handed over the sealed message I am carrying to His Majesty, I can not myself judge whether or no it will need his immediate attention. I can say no more, as you will understand. I should await the royal couple in a private room, I think, rather than here in the corridor. I did not wish to interrupt their preparations for dinner by going to their apartment at this hour."

So when King Arnold, Queen Tabitha and their attendants appeared, Louise intercepted the King, spoke quietly to him and led him to a small sitting room. Said the Queen, "Business once more, I guess, my dear. Should we proceed into dinner or would you prefer us to wait for you?" King Arnold shook his head, saying, "Please offer my apologies to the gathering, my sweet. I shall be as quick as I can, depending on the seriousness of the matter, of course."

Once in the sitting room, the King took a seat, accepted the sealed scroll from Sir Lionel, and when Louise made to leave, said, "No, no, my dear, I have no secrets from you, but in any case, let me first see what is in this mysterious document. It has not a sender's name inscribed, so from whom does it come, Sir Lionel?"

"Well, my liege, it was given me early this morning at a meeting of several of your barons at Winchester, that I believe was convened by Lord Hoxteth, the one whose duty it was to raise forces for your crusade, and it was he who handed me this missive – but he gave no indication to me of its content or import."

"So let me see," said the King, unsealing and unrolling the parchment and pursing his lips as he scanned down what appeared to be a lengthy document.

"It is indeed signed 'Hoxteth of Warrington', with half a dozen co-signatories. It takes on the characteristics of a petition and opens with a statement that I shall read out. 'If it please Your Majesty, we, your loyal Barons, have no intent to imply that we are in any wise discontented with your Majesty's actions and commands, but merely wish you to be aware of certain mutterings among the troops who have been already recruited for the Holy Land.' Well, well, what is this all about? I will read it closely before I comment further. Maybe I shall need to seek independent advice before I am done, so could Vincent Crabbe be sent for, please, as I have often found him capable of striking quickly to the heart of knotty matters!"

Louise rang for a footman and sent him off with a few murmured instructions. Meanwhile, King Arnold read on, with his expression hinting, in succession, at amusement, puzzlement, despair and finally at barely contained anger. He finished reading and almost threw the scroll down on the table in front of him, just as Vincent hurried in.

"Now, my lady, Mr Crabbe, and Sir Lionel, we have here a situation that will take a deal of teasing out. Here are its main parts. Point the first – some of the soldiery believe that they are being treated unfairly according to their place of origin, with troops from the South and East being favoured over those of the middle shires, the North and the West."

"Point the second – there are some who claim that this unfairness has come about due to the asking and granting of monetary rewards, in particular that some of those with rich agricultural holdings have been buying off their recruits so that they may proceed with harvesting, while others have had their labour forces stretched to breaking."

"And, point the third," Arnold went on, looking disconsolate, "the barons who feel hard done by are threatening to defy my royal edicts, since it has been rumoured that I have treated some who have refused to provide these services with leniency."

Vincent spoke up now, "Your Majesty, may I plead with you to resist any temptation to immediate, even impulsive, reaction. What I believe is needed is a thorough examination of the facts of the matter, rather than conjecture. In my view, convening a council of barons might be a wise step to take."

Chapter 36

King Arnold shrugged and drew himself up. "You are right, my friend! But all this will have to wait for the morrow. Now, Sir Lionel, since it is much too late for you to ride back to Winchester tonight, please join us at table. In the morning I will draft a missive for you to take to the palace comptroller, Lord Delves, but for now, let us return to celebrating dear Beatrice's birthday!"

And indeed, the festivities were taken up with great enthusiasm by all present. Following the banquet, a group of musicians, directed by Guillaume du Boise, opened the ball with a selection of lively dance tunes, and soon all those who enjoyed dancing were whisking their partners around or taking their places in elaborate cinque-paces, courantes or allemandes.

Those fond of less energetic pursuits soon fell into small groups for conversation, and, inevitably, in the corners of the ballroom, card games were joined by devoted enthusiasts of that pastime, while a succession of maids distributed cool drinks to all.

And then, during a lull in activity, as Mr Pemberton the majordomo struck his staff on the floor for silence, Lady Louise arose.

"My dearest friends, relations and acquaintances, I thank you for attending this event today. It is, of course, part of the celebration of my dear daughter's coming-of-age, but I have also to point out that it marks a number of other important turning points. As most of you are already aware, their Majesties the King and Queen will soon be taking Woodhampton Castle as their principal residence and the seat of their reign, a very notable transition. And you all know that my son, Brendan, will follow his monarch's direction to leave this country before long – we all have mixed feelings about this, but we must accept it as a political necessity, and I for one feel no rancour towards King Arnold over the affair."

"I have one further announcement to make and I deem this to be a proper occasion. I shall very soon depart this castle, hand over my responsibilities for running it to the royal staff and retire to my late parents' mansion at Chelsfield Hall, where my lifestyle will become one much more suitable for an elderly lady who is not so energetic as she once was. My daughter,

Lady Beatrice, and my almost adopted son, dear Vincent Crabbe, will stay on here, since the King and Queen have persuaded them both to take on roles as advisors to the royal court – and, besides, Vincent could never be persuaded to part with his bees for very long!"

There was general applause from the company at this speech, and Louise was seen to dab some tears from her cheek as she withdrew to resume her seat at the card-table with Elfrida Duchess of Dorset, Lady Hermione Bagshott and the Landgravine Konstanze of Hesse.

As promised, after breakfast the next morning, King Arnold summoned Sir Lionel to his apartment, where he and Vincent had been conferring over the compilation of a document.

Said the King, "We have been careful to maintain a business-like air in this missive, being neither accusatory nor justificatory. I wish to be firmly in control when we meet the Barons at Winchester in seven days' time, a delay which should provide sufficient opportunity for all those concerned or interested to gather at the palace. Vincent has agreed to take part in the talks as a formal interlocutor, enabling him to give his powers of veracity full rein. Woe betide any participant who might have it in his mind to dissemble at his questions!"

"I have addressed the document to Lord Delves, the comptroller of the palace, rather than replying to Lord Hoxteth's dispatch – which, by the way, I regard as somewhat of an impertinence – and I have asked him to convene a group of those who, following Hoxteth, have made open or implied criticisms of my decisions in the matter of Lord Musgrave, as well as being sure to invite a number of those notables who have maintained disinterest, or at least have kept their own counsel. We shall see!"

Sir Lionel took the document, rolled it and sealed it and placed it in his pouch, slung over his shoulder. "I will convey this to Winchester with all speed, my liege. Before noon, matters should be in train. I shall of course, over the next few days, keep you fully informed of developments. It may be that you will be sent further missives, which I will bring you without delay."

The courier saluted and left, with his aide, to take horse to Winchester.

"Now," said the King, "Tabitha and I will have to decide when we should return to Winchester. We need not go immediately, but I would like to give myself at least a couple of days there before the council is convened, so that I may make my own discreet enquiries before the confrontation. Would you be happy to accompany me, Vincent?"

"Certainly, Your Majesty, and I should like to point out that, if it should prove desirable for you to visit other royal establishments, such as that in London, we have the power to dream ourselves anywhere very swiftly – and, I might add, completely inconspicuously! When there is already a smell of conspiracy in the air, honest men need not feel they have an obligation to broadcast their actions to all and sundry."

And so, after two days, the royal couple, accompanied by Vincent – and Beatrice too, who said that she was certainly not going to miss any opportunity for action – boarded the coach and set off on the road to Winchester with a guard of six troopers. Several household officials who had come from the palace this time would be staying in Woodhampton to assist in the continuing preparations for the move from Winchester.

The journey was easy and rapid, and it was early afternoon when the coach pulled up in the forecourt of Winchester Castle. A group of senior officials greeted the King and Queen, including Lord Delves and his secretary. As the Queen and the others went inside, the comptroller took King's arm and led him and Vincent to his main bureau, where he asked the pair to sit down and rang for someone to bring refreshments.

"Your Majesty," he said quietly and seriously, "I have to inform you of further developments since you last heard from me. When I informed Hoxteth that you desired a meeting, which you had commanded would include others than his immediate coterie, he began to bluster, turning red in the face. It is my belief that he had assumed that he had your ear exclusively. If you will forgive me saying so, Sire, I also have the impression that he takes you for a simpleton! He is a dyed-in-the-wool military man and perhaps he mistakes reason for weakness."

"So," replied the King, "this confirms my suspicions that Hoxteth and his crew have an axe of their own to grind. We shall have to proceed with caution, but I believe the majority of the nobility are loyal to the royal house. If we can expose a few as plotters or even traitors they can be dealt with straightly."

Chapter 37

Lord Delves continued, "I have taken the liberty, Sire, of speaking to a small group of nobles and palace officials who are undoubtedly loyal, so that we may, if you wish, discuss our strategies together. We anticipated that you would arrive some time today, so they have been prepared to take luncheon with you in your private dining room whenever it is convenient."

King Arnold clasped Delves' hand warmly, saying, "It is a great comfort for a monarch to have such stout friends. So often the burden of a reign can fall heavily on a single pair of shoulders. Together we should form a strong enough alliance that will dispose of these threats, if threats they truly are. Let us join them for this luncheon in an hour; meanwhile I will speak to the Queen and Lady Beatrice and we shall decide what parts, if any, they desire to play as this drama unfolds."

In the royal dining room were six men and two ladies, and Lord Delves introduced Vincent and Beatrice to each of them in turn, explaining that they were the King's personal advisers and had particular qualities and talents that would be especially valuable when the time came to interrogate Lord Hoxteth and his associates. Queen Tabitha had decided not to be involved in that confrontation.

"But first," said King Arnold, taking his seat and signalling the others to follow suit, "we need to consider the situation and examine our alternative courses of action, whatever we might find necessary. If Hoxteth is simply carrying out what he deems to be his duty, that is one thing. But if we detect a scent of conspiracy about him and his companions – and Lady Beatrice and Mr Crabbe will soon be able to find this out, using their special talents – then we must hold ourselves ready to take whatsoever decisive, or even forceful, action is called for."

One of the ladies, the Countess Irena of Luxemburg, explained that she had asked to join this meeting because, as the spouse of the ambassador of that Duchy to the court at Winchester, she was aware of somewhat similar disquiet about recruitment for the crusades among her compatriots, saying "Any actions taken here by you, Your Majesty, will doubtless serve as useful guides for us. I have put myself forward today because my husband is not in England at present."

There followed some discussion about ways and means, but for the most part this was merely a matter of conjecture, producing no fresh ideas, so after an hour or so, King Arnold thanked everyone for their support and adjourned the meeting. "I have been reassured that I can rely on some steady allies, and for that I am grateful. We shall meet again – let it be tomorrow at noon – when we shall prepare to catechize Lord Hoxteth. I will command Hoxteth and his crew to attend us at one of the clock."

At the appointed hour, the Council of Barons was assembled in rows behind a table, with the King at its centre, and Beatrice and Vincent to his left and right. Lord Delves met Hoxteth and his three companions outside the door, and then led them to stand facing the table, with a line of the King's guards standing against the wall behind them. It had been suggested by Vincent that this arrangement would create a sense of discomfort, preventing Hoxteth from taking the initiative. "I believe that his usual custom is to adopt an aggressive stance, so we should not make it too easy for him to do this," Vincent said.

Accordingly, King Arnold opened the meeting by giving the names and stations of his advisors, and then asked Hoxteth to introduce his supporters in his turn, explaining that first he, then Mr Crabbe and Lady Beatrice would each put a single question to him and receive his response.

He then asked Hoxteth the first question, "So, my lord, you made a number of claims in the dispatch you sent me by the hand of Sir Lionel Fitz-Harris, my courier. Do you still maintain their truth?"

"Why, certainly, Your Majesty, and I will relate them again, should you wish this."

"That will not be necessary, but we do have further questions for you. My advisor, Mr Vincent Crabbe, will start this process. Vincent, your question, please."

Vincent had taken scant notice of the glib assurance that Hoxteth had just given to the King, who did not have the advantage of the gift of veracity, so he made sure that his own question would be truly testing.

"Lord Hoxteth, please tell me, are you completely loyal to the King, and is your chief concern the safety of your monarch, or do you have a personal motive for making these charges?"

The effect of this question on Hoxteth was immediate and astounding – his eyes bulged, the veins on his forehead stood out, and, instead of replying, he fell to the ground in a deep swoon. Beatrice stepped forward and rested her hand on his temple.

"He lives!" she exclaimed, "But his mind could not withstand the turmoil that Vincent's question awakened, when he realized that he was compelled to condemn himself. He will not regain his wits for some time – I suggest he be taken away to a place where he can be watched carefully and, if necessary, restrained. It is quite possible that he could do himself harm to avoid answering the question, which would inevitably reveal his treachery. Now I will ask his companions some questions of my own."

Under her interrogation, Hoxteth's associates soon admitted that there had in fact been no general objection from the barons to recruiting their men for the Crusades. Some of those lords had pointed out that there would be some hardships, but accepted that these were the inevitable outcomes of going to war. The group showed themselves to be not as adamant as Hoxteth, and grudgingly admitted their own culpability in the affair, while assuring the King that they wished him no harm and vowed their loyalty to the throne, saying that they been misled by Hoxteth when he told them he was acting properly.

Said King Arnold, "You shall not go unpunished – you must be held responsible for your actions whether or not you were persuaded by that dominant figure – so you will be taken hence and imprisoned while I receive advice as to a suitable penalty. As for Lord Hoxteth, he will bear the full weight of the law since he is clearly guilty of treason for attempting to influence my rule over the kingdom through falsehoods and deceit. I have my guards waiting ready to take you all away."

As the bedraggled group was hustled out of the room, King Arnold gave a huge sigh, embraced Beatrice and Vincent, and thanked them with tears welling up in his eyes. "Let us go and tell Tabitha of this," he said, "she will be mightily relieved. She puts on a brave face, as befits a Queen of England, but beneath that she is a woman and a loving wife."

Chapter 38

The King decided that it was his duty to stay in Winchester until the trial of Lord Hoxteth and his minions could take place, but insisted that Queen Tabitha, Beatrice and Vincent return to Woodhampton, saying, "It is regrettable that we have been forced to deal with this predicament, but I believe it will very shortly be resolved. I will myself rejoin you, dear Beatrice, to continue celebrating your birthday, just as soon as I can. Thanks to the efforts of Lord Delves, we have already a sufficient number of barons at Winchester to constitute a quorum of the House of Lords, the highest court of the land, which will administer justice to these wretches. I shall demand that it be convened with as little delay as possible. Once again, treachery against the royal house of England has been forestalled by the efforts of you, Lady Beatrice, and your friend Vincent, just as they were so many years ago by you two and by Beatrice's mother, the Lady Louise."

Beatrice thanked the King and prepared to leave, but paused long enough to assure King Arnold that should she or Vincent be required to give evidence or for any further interrogations, they would be standing ready to be summoned back to Winchester at short notice.

Tabitha, Beatrice and Vincent dream-travelled back to Woodhampton, where they were enthusiastically welcomed and bombarded with questions, by Louise, Konstanze and the others. As Ruprecht remarked, "There is no doubt that the duties of those who rule are all-embracing and demanding. I have realized this of myself, even though my own domain of Hesse is but an insignificant fragment compared with the Kingdom of England. I'm sure we are all awaiting the outcome of the trial with keen interest, whenever it might be resolved."

Said Queen Tabitha, "I, of course, am on tenterhooks also. I have decided that I will dream myself to Winchester briefly each day to see my dear husband and to discover how matters are proceeding. I shall not go today – that would be premature – but I shall travel thence tomorrow evening, after another of Woodhampton's magnificent banquets."

Fritzi announced that she and Clotilda would take the opportunity to visit their Hastings shop, taking Roswitha and

Angela Sonderhoff along too, to show them the place and to see what else the town of Hastings had to offer. They would travel by carriage, to give their companions a taste of the English countryside, Fritzi saying that they would probably take luncheon while in Hastings.

After the unwelcome excitement of the last few days, all the other guests and residents were only too keen to fall back into their rounds of recreational pursuits, to which had been added, at the suggestion of young Wilfred, a competition for the pets of all the children of the castle and estate. Many little boys and girls brought along kittens, hens, puppies, rabbits and even a kid goat that belonged to little Winnie. "Now I realize where her liking for goats comes from!" remarked Louise.

But the pet that excited the greatest interest – and apprehension in some of the audience – was a large grass-snake brought along by none other than Denise du Boise. She was at great pains to point out to everybody who was reluctant to touch it that it was neither venomous nor slimy, and she was able to persuade some of the other children to take it in their hands, or even drape it around their necks, to the accompaniment of much nervous giggling.

Vincent was appointed as chief judge of the event, and he managed to devise such a diverse number of categories and classes that almost every pet qualified for a prize. The prize for the smallest pet, for instance, was won by a snail belonging to a toddler from the village, while that for the pet that was hardest to stroke was shared between a stickleback fish in a bucket and a hedgehog. Beatrice was in charge of the prize-giving, and made sure that she selected prizes that were suitable and not so elaborate that they would spark envy in the other children.

After this pet show, the children themselves competed with one another in a number of novelty races, such as sack races, three-legged races and egg-and-spoon races. The one that brought the greatest hilarity was the wheelbarrow race, during which the child acting as the wheelbarrow invariably collapsed onto the grass as the pusher attempted to extract the maximum speed from him or her.

And then, of course, everyone was ready for a selection of cool drinks, cakes and other tidbits, which had been set out in a marquee in the gardens.

While the children were all enjoying themselves, under the affectionate supervision of Vincent and Beatrice, the other adults were whiling away the time by playing cards, it being a little chilly outside for aught but energetic pursuits. Ruprecht and Konstanze were showing themselves to be a formidable combination at French ruff, to the frustration of their opponents, Louise and Elfrida, even though they were constantly encouraged by Hermione, when she was not excusing herself from time to time and popping out to make sure that Brendan and Florence were "not getting up to anything!"

As dusk approached, the card party broke up and everyone retired to their apartments to make themselves ready for dinner, which that night would be fairly modest by Woodhampton standards, a full banquet being promised for the next day, when it would accompany a grand ball.

Beatrice was with her Mama in her bedroom, where they were selecting outfits that would not prematurely reveal the special dresses they would wear at the ball on the morrow. As they chatted, Louise suddenly paused and held her head in an enquiring posture, as though she could hear something.

Beatrice, somewhat alarmed, laid her hand on her mother's arm. Louise turned to her and reassured her, "There is nothing amiss, my darling, but I have a strong feeling that there has been a significant happening at Winchester. Maybe one of us should quickly dream travel there to discover what is going on."

"By the way, this reminds me that, although I have bestowed some powerful magic gifts upon you, you have not yet attained the full powers of a wise woman like myself, including the one of second sight that I have just experienced. Before long, we must remedy this – I must not risk going to my grave before bequeathing you the entire panoply."

Beatrice hugged Louise and left, saying, "I will collect Vincent and we shall go to Winchester immediately. If we are late getting back for dinner, please make our excuses to everyone. We shall let you know with dispatch what has transpired at the palace, if indeed it is of any significance."

She swept out of the room and headed for Vincent's apartment, allowing a concerned expression to return to her face as soon as she had left her mother.

Chapter 39

Beatrice and Vincent swiftly dreamed themselves to the royal apartments of Winchester Castle, where in the anteroom they discovered Lord Delves in conversation with Sir Lionel Fitz-Harris, the Royal Messenger. As they became visible, Delves came forward and grasped Vincent by both shoulders, saying, "I am indeed glad to see you, Mr Crabbe, and Lady Beatrice too, as there has just occurred an event that concerns you both; had you not appeared so fortuitously I would have sent Sir Lionel to inform you."

"So, please tell us," said Beatrice, "is King Arnold safe and well? My Mama, Lady Louise, has sensed, but a half-hour since, that some incident of great importance had happened here, which is why we have come."

"His Majesty is indeed in no danger, I am glad to assure you. No, it is Lord Hoxteth, who, I am astonished to say, has met with a terrible fate – terrible for him, but maybe not so terrible for us! Please take a seat, and I will relate to you what has recently transpired."

"After the interrogation at which you two performed so outstandingly, Lord Hoxteth was placed, still unconscious, on a cot in a store-room on this floor, guarded outside by a captain and a serjeant, as befitted his rank. They reported to me from time to time, on every occasion saying that he appeared to be unconscious or asleep. The other accused persons were taken to cells in the palace guardhouse, where they too were watched over, but by ordinary soldiers."

Lord Delves, who was evidently still in a state of some excitement, paused at this point and mopped his brow with a kerchief.

"About an hour ago, the watchers outside heard a commotion in the room, so quickly unlocking the door, they burst in, to encounter a scene of horror. Hoxteth was hanging from the bars of the high window – he had twisted some bed-linen into a rope – and his face was black. The serjeant cut the noose with his dagger and the two laid the prisoner on the bed, where it soon became obvious that there remained no life in the body!"

"We sent to inform King Arnold immediately, of course, but discovered that he had left the palace for a carriage drive in the local countryside. His doctors had advised him to take as much rest as possible, saying that he should try to return to the relaxed airs of Woodhampton, rather than staying here, but he insisted that his duties lay in Winchester until the trial of the conspirators was successfully prosecuted. I anticipate that he will return shortly from this excursion; he was accompanied by two of his aides and a small detachment of soldiers."

"Well, my Lord," said Vincent, "I commend you for keeping your composure till now, but really we can do nothing more until the King returns. I assume that there is no pressing need to remove the body – tell me, does the late Lord Hoxsteth have a wife and family who need to be informed of his demise?"

Lord Delves pondered a little and then said, "I'm ashamed to admit that I know not. He conducted himself always so much in the role of a serving soldier that I believe he never felt it necessary to mention anything of a personal nature. Who would know?"

Beatrice then spoke up, "In my experience, it is always amongst those below stairs that there is endless gossip concerning both the private and the public affairs of every notable denizen of a household, or visitors to it, for that matter. I see no reason why Winchester Castle should be an exception. Let us send for the chatelaine!"

A footman was dispatched and soon returned with Mistress Maitland, a craggy lady with a permanent frown on her brow. She curtseyed to Lord Delves and soon vouchsafed the answer to his question, that Lord Hoxteth was certainly not married, and as far as she knew had little to do with his brother and sisters, who all lived in the North – in Lancashire, she thought. When she begged to enquire the reason for Lord Delves' interest, she was told only that Lord Hoxteth was deceased, not the manner of his passing.

Late in the afternoon, King Arnold returned from his excursion and was sat down in his sitting room by Lord Delves to hear the news. He was very quiet for a while, and then spoke.

"I suppose I should be very pleased that I no longer have to deal with a traitor, nonetheless I cannot do otherwise than feel sad that a fellow-creature has been driven to this extreme. I think that the least we can do is give him a Christian funeral –

but the Church will insist that he, as a suicide, not be buried in consecrated ground. Let us be grateful that he had no close family."

Said Lord Delves, "But what of his confederates? Should we proceed with their trial before the House of Lords?"

"Oh, certainly!" was the King's reply. "They are no less culpable for the fact that their leader has been eliminated. But, if you will pardon me, Delves, I will leave all this to you, for I am become suddenly very weary, and long to resume my holiday at Woodhampton – is there not to be a grand banquet and ball there tomorrow evening? Perhaps Vincent and Beatrice will do me the service of dream carrying me there, as soon as we have taken a little nourishment!"

While at the table, Beatrice asked the King whether the passing of Hoxteth would have any effect on Brendan's circumstances. "This question has occurred to me also," said he, "I will have to take constitutional and legal advice, but at the least, I can see that I might be enabled to reduce his period of exile to a few years only – leave it with me, and I will come to a decision in the next few weeks."

When they arrived back at Woodhampton, the first thing that King Arnold did was to seek out Queen Tabitha and apprise her of the recent dramatic events. He gave leave to Vincent and Beatrice to spread the same news in whatever way they thought meet, to anyone who had any interest in it. This caused, of course, a wave of speculation to spread throughout the castle, and particularly interested Euphemia, Konstanze and Ruprecht.

Ruprecht said, "It may be that, because of these developments, Brendan and Florence will be allowed to return to England earlier than they thought, but I should like to make it clear that they will still be as welcome as ever to spend whatever time they need or desire at Schloss Kirschbaum with us. And it goes without saying that our castle is still to be regarded as a second home for our dear friends Louise, Beatrice and Vincent. Now, I feel the pangs of hunger rising – let us all go in to dinner – with the permission of our hosts, of course!"

Over dinner there was but one item of conversation, with speculation of all sorts arising as to the fate of the co-conspirators, the outcomes for Brendan and his bride-to-be, and whether there would be implications for the recruitment for the crusades.

Chapter 40

Vincent awoke early the next morning to the sound of tapping at his door. Calling out "Come in," he got out of bed and wrapped himself in a robe and saw that it was Clive, who was acting as deputy stable-master while Potter was away in Schloss Kirschbaum.

"I'm sorry to disturb you so early, Mr Crabbe," said he, "but all of us down there are puzzled and worried about the animals, not only the horses, but the dogs, too. In the middle of the night they started behaving like they were frightened of something – trampling about and whinnying or barking. The dogs have their tails between their legs and are cowering as though they have been whipped, even Her Majesty's Joris and Hero, who are usually impossible to upset."

"Thank you, Clive, "said Vincent, "give me a few moments to get dressed and I will join you in the stables and we'll see whether I can find out anything more – you know that I can commune with animals in their own tongues."

As Vincent crossed the yard to the stables he could hear that the horses were still disturbed; some of them were crashing about in their stalls and whinnying. As Clive and he went in, Vincent raised his voice and gave a long neighing call. The horses were immediately quieter, and the dogs in the adjacent kennels also stopped barking. He approached one of the horses that he knew well, put his hands on his neck and spoke softly to him in horse language, to which the horse readily replied.

Turning to Clive, Vincent told him what had been said. "This steed tells me that he and his companions heard a strange sound in the night, at first distant, but then seeming to approach. The horse had difficulty in explaining what it was like, this sound, as it was outside his normal experience and he had no words for it, but I got the impression it might have been a low roaring or howling. He says they can still hear it, and it seems to be just outside the castle, but I can hear nothing, can you, Clive? Let me see if a dog will give a similar account."

He went to Joris' kennel and knelt down so he could put his face near that of the dog, and started a low-pitched conversation, from time to time patting him in encouragement. He straightened up and explained, "Joris has much the same story as the horse, but with one notable difference – he says that the roaring, or whatever it is, sounds to him like a human speaking at a very low pitch, or so I understood. What he actually said was that the voice was like that of a huge giant, as much different from a man as a man is from a little child!"

"What I can't understand, Mr Crabbe," said Clive, "is why we cannot hear it if the animals can. I never thought of a horse, or even a dog, as having much keener hearing than a person, did you, sir?"

"This is puzzling to me, too," replied Vincent, "I wonder if other animals can hear it as well. Can you find a cat for me – I know we keep a number around the castle, whose duty is keeping the rats and mice under control. No, wait – let us find Wilfred, I have a better idea."

By this time, the population of the castle was beginning to get up and about, and Clive sent one of his stable-hands to find Wilfred. He soon came back with the lad, who was still rubbing his eyes and yawning.

Vincent explained what was afoot, and Wilfred immediately brightened up and looked interested, saying, "What must I do, Mr Vincent, do you want me to change my shape?"

"Yes, my boy, in fact I might want you to try several different forms. And if you can hear this noise at all, you might be able to tell us much more about it than the horses and dogs are able to do. You could start off as a dog, since we know that Joris heard this sound. First see whether you can hear it, and then I hope you will be able to tell us more. Meanwhile, I will get word to Lady Beatrice, lest she should feel left out of the matter, and I will also go and see whether Lady Louise can help – her experience of magic is much superior to mine, and I feel certain that there is magic involved here in some way."

Before long, indeed, both ladies were standing expectantly by the kennels, hearing the accounts of Clive and Vincent, while Wilfred, in the guise of a shaggy terrier, cocked his head to one side and another, from time to time licking his nose. Then, seeing that Beatrice and Louise had arrived and were waiting, Wilfred regained his shape as a boy.

"Well," he said, "I could certainly hear this sound – it did not seem particularly loud to me, but I realize that we humans do not have as keen hearing as some of our four-footed friends, so even though I was a dog, perhaps this was still the case. But, apart from the loudness, I was able to pick out human speech! That is why I listened so long, I was trying to get meaning from what was being called out."

"And were you able to do this?" asked Beatrice, while Louise excitedly nodded too.

"Yes, my lady, and I can tell you now that the poor creature, whatever or whoever it be, is extremely distressed! What I could hear it saying, over and over again, was 'Help me; get me out! I need to be free!' and similar appeals, but I did not try to answer – I thought that Lady Louise might have some better ideas than I about what should be said."

Louise replied, "You are right, Wilfred, my boy. As you all know, I am a wise woman, and I have had encounters with many different enchanters and enchantments over the years. Beatrice may recall how I released her first little beagle from his porcelain prison when we were in Schloss Kirschbaum a long time ago. I am convinced that what we have here is a similar story; a poor soul is entrapped somehow, but in what form and where, we do not yet know. However, we have the aid of Wilfred and a pair of clever dogs to help us in our hunt. Come, let us go out into the demesne and find out whether we can track down the source of these plaintive cries for help."

"What we need, Mama," said Beatrice, "is for our brave Wilfred to transform into some creature or other that uses its particularly acute sense of hearing to find its prey, or to locate other sources of sound. I have heard that some bats are able to find their way in dark caves in such ways – does anyone know whether this be true or no?"

Wilfred had a worrisome thought about this, "Are not bats blind in the daylight – this is what we are always told. I have certainly seen them swooping among trees in the woods at night, catching insects, I suppose."

"Well," said Louise, "we can combine our talents, then. If Vincent allows Wilfred the bat to hang from his finger, since bats like to hang upside-down, then he can do the seeing, and Wilfred can do the listening! Are you agreeable to this, Wilfred? Well then, off we go! How will you tell us which way you want us to walk, Wilfred?"

"Why, I shall just turn my head and look in that direction!"

Chapter 41

The little party set off almost immediately, first into the gardens, where Wilfred shook his little head as they tried every corner. Beatrice then remembered that there was a way into the woods beyond the vegetable plots, so suggested they might try in that direction. But they had not travelled very far before the bat Wilfred again shook his head, even more vigorously than before, so they came back into the garden, with the idea of circling the castle, especially along the wall of the stable yard. Joris and Hero were trotting along after them, and as they rounded a corner of the castle and started to cross the green in front of the main gate, both dogs stopped and raised their heads, sniffing the air and turning this way and that.

Vincent asked what they had heard, and Joris told him that the sound was becoming much louder now. Vincent held up his hand, almost as though Wilfred were a lantern that he wanted to use to scan the grounds, and was rewarded by the bat opening his leathery wings a little and nodding his head. And then Louise stopped and raised both her arms, saying, "I am beginning to hear it myself, now!" In some excitement, she led them across the green, almost breaking into a run, until they stood in front of what Beatrice recalled had at one stage been a pillar holding the bell that in former times was sounded morning and night when the castle gates were opened or closed. Now it was no more than a moss-covered pile of tumbled masonry, but as they reached it, both dogs became very excited and sniffed and scratched at its base, while Wilfred dropped to the ground and regained his natural form.

Louise motioned her companions to stand back, approached the pile with her arms raised and intoned a long chant in a language that not even Vincent nor Beatrice could follow. She then picked up a stone from the foot of the pile and struck the pillar thrice, uttering strange words after each impact. She withdrew a yard or so and, as everyone watched in rapt attention, a large crack appeared in the pillar and four or five masonry blocks were pushed out by something or someone inside, who then stumbled, blinking, into the open.

The figure was revealed to be that of a man, short and stocky, with long white hair flowing to waist-length and draped in filthy sackcloth. He approached Louise and, falling to his knees, made humble obeisance. She put her hands on his shoulders to comfort him and told him he had nothing to fear, that he was now among friends. "Come with us, and we shall make you comfortable, are you thirsty and hungry? When you have settled yourself, you shall tell us your story. I am Louise, and these are Beatrice, Vincent and Wilfred. And, of course, these dogs are our faithful Joris and Hero. Can you tell us your name now?"

The man licked his dry lips and his croaking speech was halting, "I am called, or was once called, Sir Cedric Athelstane, and I used to be a warrior for hire."

An hour later, Sir Cedric having been ministered to by castle staff, bathed and dressed in decent clothes, with his hair trimmed, and having been persuaded to eat a light meal, joined Louise, Beatrice and Vincent in Louise's sitting room. Said Lady Louise, "Now, Sir Cedric, if you are ready, perhaps you could relate to us the events which led to your predicament and subsequent captivity. Can you bear to tell us about it?"

"Well, my lady," he replied, and his voice was already stronger, "as far as I can judge it must all have happened some fourteen years since. I say this with some confidence, because my oppressor's last words to me, which I can still hear ringing in my ears, were to the effect that I would not see the light of day again for seven years and then for seven more. At that time, King Adelbert was on the throne; I was just told that he died a few years ago, but I do not know yet why he was succeeded by King Arnold and not by his son, Prince Godfrey. While I was being looked after just now, I was given a lot of chatter by the servants, but I could not take all of it in."

"Since I was first entombed, I am thankful to say that I have been in a deep sleep; had I been conscious, I doubt that I could have borne the experience so long. As it is, when I awoke – it must have been but a few hours ago – the terror of my confinement must have driven me out of my mind were it prolonged an hour longer."

He appeared to cast his mind back those few hours, and waves of disgust, anger and sheer panic seemed to cross his face one after another. He drew himself together and took up his narrative.

"My first thought was to call for help, and so I did, but I had no way of knowing whether or no I was being heard. But I have always had a stubborn nature, and so I persisted. So you can imagine my relief when I heard someone outside my prison call out in a language I knew not. At that, I felt myself strengthen, and then, hearing blows outside, I pushed aside the stones. The result you all saw!"

Said Beatrice, "We are all so glad that we were able to help. I should say that this was mainly because my Mama, Lady Louise, is truly a wise woman, and she deserves most of your thanks. But we are all agog – at least I am – to hear what brought you to your predicament! Mama believes that you were not merely imprisoned, but enchanted."

"Of course!" said Louise, "If he had merely been confined by stones, he would not have survived a week – so the enchantment had its benefits as well as its horrors! So, Sir Cedric, if you will, please tell us what chain of events led you to this pass. You need not relate all the story at once, we have plenty of time – perhaps you could start by telling us who it was that enchanted you, if indeed, you know this."

Sir Cedric closed his eyes as he made an effort to recall it, "Oh, yes, my lady, I do know who it was, and it still makes my blood run cold to call her to mind – she is the only truly evil being I have ever had the misfortune to encounter. Her name is – or was, since I know not whether she still exists – Lady Fafnirsdottir, which I was told means 'daughter of the dragon'. She was certainly more fierce than any ordinary woman I have ever known."

Hearing this, Louise gave a sharp cry, and sat down suddenly on the couch. Recovering her calm, she said, "A long time since, I heard of this witch, but I knew not that she had ever come to England; her home was reputed to be in the lands of ice and snow, far to the north. I hope with all my heart that by now she has returned thither! Please continue, Sir Cedric, I should not have interrupted you. How was it that she came to enchant you, was she called up by an enemy of yours, or did you offend her in some way?"

"Well, my lady," said Sir Cedric, with a puzzled look on his face, "I really cannot say whether it was the work of an enemy – I certainly had nothing to do with her before she hurled abuse at me and cast me into that prison!"

Chapter 42

Sir Cedric seemed to ponder a little, and then continued, "Perhaps it would be best if I try to relate the events that immediately preceded my confrontation with the sorceress. It all took place not many leagues from here, in a manor-house called Bramwell Hall."

At this, both Louise and Beatrice sat up and paid even more intense attention. Beatrice seemed about to speak, but, at a look from her mother, decided to keep quiet for the moment.

"I had been summoned there," went on the knight, "because the tenant of the manor, the Earl of Bickley, had got into some dispute or other and wished to engage my services – he told me frankly that he wanted me to do someone harm. As I have said before, at that time I was offering myself as a warrior for hire, a disreputable profession that is sometimes taken up in times of peace by former soldiers who find themselves with no other source of income. At my lowest ebb, I had even been forced to resort to breaking windows, setting fire to haystacks, stealing carriages and other shameful activities altogether unworthy of a decent man. But all of those are preferable to what I uneasily predicted would be asked of me next – to injure or even kill someone."

"When I first arrived at the Hall," he continued, "I was taken to a meeting room furnished with a long table surrounded by chairs and shown to a seat facing a gentleman who I took to be the Earl, who was flanked by two people, a middle-aged secretary with a pen-and-ink and a stack of paper, and a grey-faced hunchbacked woman, who I later discovered to be my ultimate nemesis, the Lady Fafnirsdottir. The Earl opened the conversation by telling me I would be expected to deal severely with an enemy of his, that I had been recommended to him as a capable and ruthless professional criminal. He then catechized me, asking about my experience in such matters, my records of success in carrying out my undertakings, whether I worked alone or with confederates, and so on. I could see that the secretary was noting my answers down. The Earl seemed to be pleased when I said I always worked alone, turning to the woman and muttering something to which she nodded."

Sir Cedric stopped, apparently recalling the meeting, and his face paled visibly – it was evident that the experience, as long ago as it was, still dominated his thoughts and moods.

Beatrice took the opportunity to interpose some questions of her own, saying, "Please, Sir Cedric, tell me if I speak out of turn, but something has occurred to me that I would like you to comment upon, while we still hold the picture of that meeting in mind. Did you, perchance, have a feeling that the Earl was acting on behalf of the witch by his side, or was he speaking entirely on his own account?"

"Well, as I said, my lady, the Earl did confer with her from time to time, seeming to seek her approval. But he was certainly the spokesman – she never spoke to me directly at all. He went on to insist that I was never to speak to anyone else of the task he would give me, and that everything would go badly for me if I dared to do that. As you might imagine, by this time I could hardly contain my curiosity – all sorts of conjectures were flooding my mind. And then he disclosed what I was to do – he wanted me to burn down that very building, along with all its occupants, a sufficient time after he and his grim companion, who he then named, had left. He said that preparations had already been made, and that bales of straw soaked in colza lamp-oil had been placed in every room and cellar below the ground floor level, so that all I would have to do was to set a light to them and make my escape."

Vincent spoke for the first time, "So he was talking of Bramwell Hall itself? Did he tell you who the occupants might be?"

"Well, of course, that was my next question, but the Earl became very angry and shouted that it was none of my concern, that he had a perfectly good reason for wanting it all done, that the people deserved to be brought to justice, and that if I knew their identities I would not hesitate to do his bidding. Besides, he said, 'If you are worried that they will act to prevent you, I assure you that they are all tied and gagged and lying in the upstairs rooms,' At this, I came close to swooning, as I tried to take in what he had said. But I recovered some of my composure, stood up and cried that I would not do such a wicked act and that he must be mad to think that any man would be so vile. That was when the witch arose and pointed at me with her trembling fingers, shrieking something I could not understand. I immediately felt as though I had been turned to stone. And then I took leave of my senses!"

Sir Cedric blanched at this recollection, and Louise went and grasped his shoulders, as he appeared to be about to collapse.

He recovered his composure, sipped a cool drink, and continued. "The next I knew, I was lying bound with ropes on the floor of an open carriage, and I could see that the other occupants were the Earl and that so-called Lady, Fafnirsdottir, who were conversing, or should I say arguing, in a language that I did not recognize. All I can say is that it was closer to one of the Norse tongues than to German, Dutch or French, all of which I had heard in my travels as a soldier. Night was falling by that time – I could see naught but the branches of an occasional tall tree on one side of the road or another. By the sound of the carriage wheels, we were traversing an unpaved country road. But then, the witch saw that I was awake, once again gestured at me with her long-nailed hands, uttered an imprecation and told me of my fate, and that was the last I knew until I regained my wits in the prison where you found me today."

Vincent congratulated Sir Cedric on his account, but said that it had raised some questions, which he would like to put to him if he felt strong enough to continue. At Sir Cedric's nod, he started. "The only reason, as far as I can see, that the evil pair should have found it necessary to bring you in to set off the fire is that they needed to establish the fact that they had no connection with the crime. If they had arranged for the occupants to be tied up, and prepared the straw-bales for the conflagration, for what other reason would they have needed someone like you to start it?"

Louise went on, "I am with you, Vincent. I have no doubt of the veracity of Sir Cedric's account of those events, but they certainly make no sense otherwise. Perhaps they had arranged to be present at some public event or other occasion, where there would be witnesses a-plenty that those two could have had nothing to do with the fire."

At this, Sir Cedric seemed about to speak, but then looked even more confused than before and covered his face with his hands.

"Pray go on!" said Louise, "You have a thought to share with us?" "Why, my lady, merely that I could not imagine what respectable gathering would have accepted the attendance of someone like her, who would repel any civilized person by her very appearance, which manifested evil in its every aspect."

Chapter 43

Vincent had a quiet word or two with Louise and Beatrice, and then thanked Sir Cedric again for his narrative, saying, "It must have been very distressing for you, sir, to relive such appalling experiences, and I would suggest that what you need now is a quiet period to recover and reacquaint yourself with modern times and present circumstances. Lady Louise has offered to make accommodation available to you here in Woodhampton Castle while you decide what you want to do next. I suppose, and hope, that you have given up any thought of taking up your former seedy occupation? Meanwhile, I imagine that you will be as interested as we are in finding out whether or not there were any repercussions from the alleged activities at Bramwell Hall of this nefarious pair, Lady Fafnirsdottir and the so-called Earl of Bickley. I can still remember that era, in general terms, and I cannot recall any excitement of the kind you have described being common knowledge at the time. Either it was kept secret, or it didn't happen as this Earl made out to you."

"Yes," added Louise, "I too am puzzled, and I shall soon start making enquiries of others who were around at that time and who may have a more detailed knowledge. I shall first ask my old friend Lord Hampshire, who was in charge of many of the arrangements at the royal court in Winchester over a period of several years, which would have included the time of your misadventures."

After making sure that Sir Cedric would be looked after by the staff in a guest apartment, Louise drew Beatrice aside and spoke to her earnestly, "Now, my dear, I am even more resolved not to let a single further hour pass before I inculcate you with all the arcane powers that I possess as a wise woman. After an interval of fourteen years, it is not likely that this Fafnirsdottir woman is still lurking in this part of the country, but we must take no chances, and she may not be the only wicked witch we need to take account of. Let us repair to my apartment straight away. I shall inform our maids that they must make sure we are not interrupted for the next several hours. It may take us until late tonight to go through all the necessary rituals and lessons."

It would not be proper to describe here the ways by which Lady Louise instilled her daughter with all her powers; suffice it to say that when they had finished, Beatrice was able to do no more than sink into a deep and happy sleep, in bed next to her Mama, which is how they were discovered the next morning when Louise's maid brought a light breakfast.

Rising with alacrity, Beatrice embraced Louise and went to the window, saying, "I expected everything to look different now, but this does not seem to be the case, Mama! Wait though, a dove has just settled on the window-sill and I find I know her name, where is her nest, and the number of her brood, which hatched only recently!"

"Yes, my dear, but you will have to learn to disregard much of this sort of knowledge, lest it swamp you with its sheer volume. This does not mean that you will stop understanding it, simply that you can choose what to remark and what to dismiss! Not all we wise women have equal skills; like everyone else, some see and hear better than others! Let us try a little test. Can you tell where Vincent is right now?"

Beatrice cocked her head to one side, as though listening, and slowly a sweet smile broke out on her face. "He is in the main dining room already, taking a hearty breakfast!"

"Well then, Beatrice, you are already a better seer than I! I can get glimpses of events both near and far, but I cannot call them to mind by deliberate effort, as I see you can! Now, as I declared yesterday, I am intent on enquiring of Lord Hampshire whether he can recall any of those untoward events at Bramwell Hall, or knows aught of an Earl of Bickley – my first conjecture is that there was no such title and that Sir Cedric's protagonist was a fraud through and through. Do you, my dear, remember Lord Hampshire sufficiently well that you would be able to locate him as you did Vincent a few moments ago?"

"I believe so, Mama, let me see." Beatrice again appeared to be listening and, as she did, a succession of expressions passed over her countenance, some apparently betokening disappointment, or disinterest in scenes that were immediately dismissed, until she smiled, nodded and turned back to Louise.

"Lord Hampshire is at his ancestral country seat, Mama; should we dream ourselves there, do you think? I believe I can find our way there, although I know not whether it be north, south or which way from here – I will simply follow my sense of his presence – can you take a chance on the new-found abilities that you have so recently given me?"

Louise's response was to smile delightedly and embrace her daughter; hand-in-hand they started the humming and were off on their dreaming journey. As they went, they could see that they were approaching the coast and soon a great mansion came into sight. They chose to appear in the entrance hall and enquired of a slightly startled footman whether Lord Hampshire would receive guests, giving him their names. The man bowed and disappeared, and in a very few minutes, Lord Hampshire appeared, approached them and embraced first Louise and then Beatrice.

"When I left Woodhampton a few weeks ago, I did not expect to see you both so soon! Welcome ladies, can I offer you some refreshment? Let us make ourselves comfortable in my sitting room and you shall tell me everything you have been doing and explain the reason for your visit, if reason there be! Of course, you are always welcome here, for any reason or none. I will send word to my lady, who will be as glad to see you as I am. I would imagine she is up, dressed and respectable by now!"

Once they were all settled, and Lord and Lady Hampshire had related some of the humdrum events of their life in retirement, Louise asked leave to ask Lord Hampshire some serious questions. She first described the astounding chronicle of the discovery of the entombed Sir Cedric, and then related his story, as he had told it to her and her companions. "What I would like to ask you, my lord, is whether you have a recollection of any such mysterious events at Bramwell Hall, some fourteen years since?"

"Well, first I can tell you that the Hall was never burnt down! As I recall it, after Bramwell was disgraced and disposed of, the mansion, now yours, was taken by Lord and Lady Burminster, mainly as a retreat for times when they wished to relax from their hectic social life in London. You may recall Arthur Burminster – he was for some years a purveyor of military supplies to the English throne and to other friendly European powers. As far as I can remember, he would have been the tenant of the Hall at the time you mention, and for several years both before and after. He passed away not five years since, and the place is now vacant and in the hands of a caretaker staff.

Chapter 44

Louise continued her questioning of Lord Hampshire, "So what puzzles me still, my lord, is the identity of the so-called Earl of Bickley – did you ever hear tell of such a person? I would think that you would have as comprehensive knowledge of the English nobility as anyone living, since it fell to you as the comptroller of Winchester at the time to peruse the credentials of every visitor to the court of King Adelbert, wasn't that so?"

"Your recollection is accurate, Louise – not only did I know of their lineage and connections, but most of them I could recognize on sight. But that name is unfamiliar to me – the man must certainly have been an imposter. But, strangely, the name Fafnirsdottir rings a faint bell with me – I have a feeling that I have encountered her somewhere, somehow, at some time! I will ask my spouse – she has often a stronger recollection of events than I. Mildred, my dear, have you been following our conversation? Know you aught of this Fafnirsdottir?"

"While you were talking, Maurice, I was racking my brains – I have an elusive idea that I may have encountered such a person, but it was some years ago and my memory is faint. Somehow there is an association with horses or deer – yes, that is it! The last I saw her she was riding in a strange carriage pulled by deer! I have the impression that the carriage was driven by a man dressed all in furs, as if he might have journeyed from a land of snow and ice."

Louise clapped her hands, "Yes, yes, she is indeed reputed to dwell far to the north, even beyond the Hebridean islands. They say there is a land in that direction, which some call Ice Land. Maybe that is her home. I earnestly hope she has returned there permanently. Her last known enchantment was of the unfortunate Sir Cedric Athelstane, but perhaps we should make searching enquiries. Beatrice, my love, it might be worth your while to exercise your new powers and attempt to visualize such a grey-haired, wizened witch, possibly in company with deer. I will make an effort to recall my last sight of her, too, which should reinforce your efforts. Try and picture her in your mind as last you saw her." Beatrice made herself comfortable on a couch and closed her eyes, while Louise and Mildred concentrated as well. But, after a while, Beatrice shook her head and opened her eyes, saying, "Nothing, Mama, nothing at all!"

Meanwhile, at Woodhampton Castle, Vincent was also making his own enquiries, first beseeching Sir Cedric to try to remember what more he could about the witch or her companion, if it would not be too upsetting a task for him. All Sir Cedric could do, however, was to repeat what he had already told, saying that he could recall no more, except that he could add a little to his description of the secretary who had been with the two when they first put their evil proposition to him, "I took no great mind of him at the time, as he played no active part in the interview, but he had one feature notable to me that I soon dismissed – he appeared to have more fingers than he ought on the hand that grasped his pen, maybe six or even seven! I saw not his left hand."

Vincent whistled, "Now this is something we can follow up! Legend has it that goblins and trolls are often endowed with extra fingers and toes – can you recall whether the false Earl was also so distinguished?" Sir Cedric replied, shaking his head, that he had no such memory.

Vincent went on, "When the ladies Beatrice and Louise return, I shall apprise them of this – it may be that they have also discovered more from their talk with Lord Hampshire. I feel encouraged, and I look forward to pursuing this quest further, with the aim of finding whether or not Lady Fafnirsdottir remains a menace to us or can be safely disregarded. I shall also ask questions of some of the downstairs staff – the kitchen and sculleries of a residence of this size are often abuzz with tales of all sorts, when the unschooled are apt to occupy their idle moments with prattle about elves and fairies, witches and wizards."

Not long afterwards, the ladies returned from their mission and passed on to Vincent what they had learned. They were as amazed as he to hear about the extra fingers of the secretary. Louise, too, thought that trolls were reputed to have more than five fingers on each hand, but she did not believe that goblins were thus endowed. The idea of making enquiries among the servants, who were predominantly drawn from simple country folk, appealed to her, and after they had partaken of luncheon – Beatrice explaining that dream travel appeared to make her ravenous more often than not – Beatrice and Vincent went down the kitchen stairs and sought out Mistress Travis, to explain to her the reason for their visit, as a courtesy, before approaching any of the staff. Mistress Travis, a no-nonsense woman, was somewhat sceptical, but said she had no objection to the questioning, "As long as you do not keep them from working diligently, sir and madam, if you please. You might try the scullery-maids first, they are the greatest gossips of all!"

The two were greeted by a hush as they entered the long dark room where a number of girls and women were working at tables and cisterns, scrubbing roasting-dishes with sand and scraping out pots and pans. Beatrice held up her hand, saying, "Do you know me? I am not here to chastise you, but to ask for your help." A tall girl stood up, wiped her hands on a rag and said, "Yes, my lady, we know you well, and we would like to help, however we can."

"Gather round, please," said Beatrice, "we shall not keep you from your work for long. What we would like to know is whether any of you have heard tell of elves, trolls or witches in this countryside. You may have heard that my Mama, Lady Louise, only yesterday rescued a gentleman from years of enchantment, right here in the castle grounds."

A group of three girls started whispering and giggling together, and then pushed one of their number forward, another saying, "Aggie, here, knows about such things – she has an auntie who people call a witch!" Aggie was obviously very shy about all this, so Beatrice took her arm and led her away from her friends, "Take your time, Aggie, tell me about it – is your aunt really a witch or is this just gossip? I know that people can be very cruel to those who seem a little different."

"Well, my lady, I have always got on with my Auntie Ivy very well, she cured a nasty place I had on my leg last year, by putting a compress of special leaves on it. Perhaps that sort of thing is what causes folk to think she is a witch. And she keeps a black cat with her in her little cottage on the woods that they say is worrisome." She stood on tiptoe and whispered in Beatrice's ear, "But there's more that I don't like to talk about in front of people."

Beatrice patted her hand and thanked her, saying "That is very interesting, Aggie, we must talk again soon."

Vincent, wanting to change the mood and take attention away from Aggie, then started to ask further questions, such as "Are there any woods or other places near here that people are frightened to go into. Are there tales about fairy dells or goblin burrows or the like?"

Chapter 45

Soon he and Beatrice were being regaled by all sorts of rumours, which they listened to respectfully, sometimes making notes in a little book that Vincent had in his pocket.

One little girl said she was frightened to go near the dene-hole, because her friends had said that an ogre lived in it. Beatrice told her that, as she and Vincent knew well, from years ago, there was nothing to worry about there, and that her friends had simply been trying to scare her.

When the stream of stories seemed to be drying up, Vincent thanked the girls and said that he would tell Mistress Travis how helpful they had been.

"Should we try to speak to anyone else now? Gardeners, for instance?" asked Beatrice, but Vincent replied that they probably had enough to work on for the moment. As they left the kitchen area, Vincent approached Mistress Travis and apologized for disturbing the routine of the household, telling her how helpful the scullery maids had been, "And young Aggie was particularly so – would you ask her to come and see Lady Beatrice and me when you can spare her again, please?"

"Certainly, sir, why don't I fetch her now, so she can accompany you to your quarters? There is no work down here today that cannot be interrupted for a while. I'll make sure she washes her hands and face first!"

When the three of them reached Louise's apartment they all sat down, and Louise rang for some refreshments, asking Aggie what she would like particularly. The girl curtseyed, red-faced, and answered, "Oh, my lady, I really fancy they little honey-cakes that they make in our bakehouse – we downstairs staff usually have to make do with the stale ones!"

When they were settled, Beatrice said, "Now Aggie, you said you had more that you wanted to tell us in private, is that so?"

"Yes, my lady, it was about my Auntie Ivy. I like her very much, so I often go to visit her in her little cottage in the woods and sometimes take her something nice we can share or other times we just chat. A while back, maybe six or seven weeks ago, I got there to find her door shut and bolted, not like it usually is. So I knocked and called out, 'cause I didn't know whether she might have gone out for something. She came to the door soon, but put her finger to her lips, as if she wanted me not to say anything. And then a harsh voice came from inside the cottage, saying 'Sister Ivy, whoever it is, send them away, we still have business!' And Auntie looked frightened and waved me away."

Said Beatrice, "Could you see who said that, Aggie?"

"No, my lady, but I had the feeling there was more than one of them. Anyway, a week or so later, I went to see Auntie again, and the door was on the latch as usual. I went in and Auntie Ivy was just the same as always, so we had a nice talk. And then I asked her about the strange visitors and she answered, 'Don't you worry about them, Aggie, I've told them I want nothing more to do with witchery or the like.' But she looked bothered, all the same, so I said no more."

Louise had another question, "Does your Aunt have many visitors, Aggie? Would she mind if I went to speak to her? I would just go by myself, so as not to overwhelm her – or maybe it might be better if I went along with you; what do you think?"

Aggie thought a little, and then her face brightened, "Well, my lady, she has sometimes spoken of you, and I know she thinks well of you, and of Lady Beatrice, too, so I suppose it would be all right to go by yourself. I'm sure she would make you welcome."

So, early the next day, Louise, Beatrice and Vincent set off through the woods, following Aggie's directions, until they found the cottage, in the middle of a dense stand of fir-trees, which created a rather sombre atmosphere. Beatrice and Vincent settled down on a fallen tree-trunk to wait just out of sight, while Louise walked up and knocked on the door.

She had expected Aunt Ivy to be an elderly woman, but she turned out to be no more than about forty years old, fit-looking with a spring in her step. She recognized Louise, welcomed her warmly and ushered her in, saying, "I somehow thought I might see you here, sooner or later! Did Aggie mention my eldritch visitors?"

Louise smiled and nodded, saying, "I see you have some second sight at least! Do you also know how I released Sir Cedric Athelstane from the enchantment of the witch

Fafnirsdottir, and how we are resolved to prevent her from repeating such wicked acts?"

"Well, my lady, the story of the enchantment and release is common knowledge by now in these parts – such stories spread fast! But, yes, I admit that I felt in my bones that I might soon be asked about that evil person, since I seem to have built a reputation among the locals as a witch. Like yourself, if I may be so bold as to say so, I would prefer to be called a wise woman."

She went on, "The visitors that Aggie came upon that day were members of Fafnirsdottir's coven, trying to enlist my support, because they feared that the powers of witches like themselves were being drained away, as more and more of the common people learn to read and write and realise that they have no need to fear or obey witches or wizards. That trio of sad souls told me, and you will be pleased to hear this, my lady, that because of these happenings, Fafnirsdottir had already decided that she would have to retreat to her native domain in the lands of snow and ice."

Louise was indeed glad to hear this and said, "Maybe you have already thought of this, dear Ivy, but I suggest that we two, with the help of my daughter Beatrice, who of course is also a wise woman, should conduct the proper rites that will help to banish these evil ones from this land. What do you say? Do you know where they abide at present?"

Then Beatrice was fetched, and with Vincent as an interested observer, the three of them cast certain herbs upon the fire and intoned cabalistic spells in chorus over a period of several hours. Finally, they all trooped seven times widdershins around the cottage and then embraced each other.

Ivy then said, with an air of satisfaction, "Now, if any of them try to come near, they will be afflicted with feelings of doom and dread, which they can only relieve by retreating."

Ivy invited Louise, Beatrice and Vincent to take some food and drink with her, and they exchanged professional tales of enchantments and other arcane activities until it was time to make their way back to the castle. Ivy said, as they left, "If I ever hear aught about the witch Fafnirsdotter, I will make sure to come and see you and tell you all about it! But I don't believe that we shall ever be bothered by her again! Thank you all!"

Chapter 46

Louise and Beatrice felt quite tired, even drained, after their efforts, and, as soon as they were back in the castle, retired to their chambers, while Vincent sought out Sir Cedric to tell him that he need not fear Fafnirsdottir more. The knight was extremely relieved to hear this, and asked what he could do to repay Lady Louise and the others for their kindness.

"Do not be overly concerned about this," said Vincent, "we are all only too glad that such an evil personage has been thwarted and will cause us no further trouble – we hope and pray! What will you do now? I am sure that you are welcome to stay here for as long as it takes you to make your plans."

Sir Cedric had apparently been pondering on his future life for some time, and said, "I shall certainly not resume my previous occupation of warrior for hire – at least not for disreputable tasks – but perhaps I could turn the same talents to something more worthwhile. I was wondering whether the King had a place on his staff for an elderly military man of some cunning. What do you say, Mr. Vincent?"

"Well, first of all, I should point out that you are really not so elderly as your age in years would indicate in the normal course of events. You were in a state of suspense for fourteen years, and I would hazard the thought that you may not have aged during that time. I will ask Lady Louise her opinion on that, since she is more acquainted with enchantments than I. And I will approach the King on your behalf if you wish."

With all the excitement, Beatrice had almost forgotten that that very evening was the occasion for the grand banquet and ball, so when Euphemia, Florence and Konstanza came to her apartment to show off their gowns, she had little time to marvel over them, but had to send her friends away in a hurry, so that her own maid could help her dress and arrange her hair. But when the gong was rung to invite everyone to the table she appeared, as well turned out as ever, with her birthday pendant glittering on her breast and flowers braided in her hair.

And even Vincent, not usually known as a particularly smart dresser, was resplendent in a new outfit, with, lined up across his chest, the badges that had been bestowed upon him by the late King Adelbert as a reward for his help in the defeat of the treacherous plotters.

As always at Woodhampton, the banquet that night was magnificent. When the King and Queen had arrived at the castle they had brought their own chefs with them, to add to the already highly competent kitchen staff, and there had been a consequent widening in the range of dishes on offer, with many recipes that were jealously guarded by their various owners.

The castle even boasted its own cellar-master now, and there was hardly a Bordeaux, Rhenish, Tuscan or Muscat wine that could not be found when requested by a particularly discriminating visitor. Most decent guests, however were less exacting, simply accepting that anything that was served at the castle would be of the best quality.

And after dinner, of course, there came the ball. Guillaume du Boise had arranged the music, as was his duty, and there were several ensembles in attendance, from small groups to accompany singing, to larger orchestras for the dancing. They were all kept very busy throughout the evening and into the night.

Beatrice, Euphemia, Florence and the other ladies were dazzling in their new ball gowns, and the gentlemen, too were dressed in the height of fashion.

It does not need to be mentioned that around the hall were many tables of keen card players, whose numbers grew during the course of the ball as the ladies, mainly, became somewhat exhausted by the vigour of their dancing.

Nobody arose very early the next day, but when they did, their talk was all of the banquet and ball, and of the conversations they had had with old friends and new acquaintances. Some of the guests stayed on for a day or two, but there came the inevitable moment when Beatrice bade farewell to the last of the invited visitors.

She turned once more to Lady Louise and said, "Well, Mama, I cannot hide the fact that my birthday celebrations have at last come to an end. I shall remember these days, weeks and months with pleasure for a long time, but it is still a little painful to realize that they are all over now. Back to the hum-drum affairs of a normal life!"

"Well, my dear," said Louise, hugging her daughter, "I do sympathize with you. But perhaps you might receive some consolation from the fact that I can now inform you that you are invited to be the chief bridesmaid, or maid of honour, at the nuptials of your brother Brendan and his beloved Florence, which has been arranged for a date not six weeks from now, here in the chapel of Woodhampton Castle. Florence's parents, the Duke and Duchess of Dorset, and I have been plotting this for the past week, and you are the first to know – apart from the happy pair themselves and Countess Hermione Bagshott, of course!"

"Oh, I accept the honour gladly, Mama – but have we enough time to have suitable dresses made? I suppose Florence has anticipated her need for a wedding dress for some time, though I must say, she has told me nothing! When shall we all start to prepare ourselves – I suppose we shall have to have rehearsals for the ceremony – who will officiate? Have I to make a speech – I shall rather enjoy that, I think!"

"Well," replied Louise, smiling at her daughter's obvious excitement, "most of the arrangements have been left, as is proper, to the parents of the bride-to-be, Elfrida and Henry Dorset. I believe they have asked the Bishop of Hastings to conduct the ceremony, but I know not whether he has yet accepted. But you in your position will have the duty of selecting all the bridesmaids and flowergirls, so you will have to think who to include and who to reject, making sure that no offence is taken, nor any jealousy set in train. Little girls, especially, can be very sensitive about these matters, as I seem to recall!"

Said Beatrice, "I must confer with Florence – she may well have some bridesmaids in mind – has she any sisters, Mama? And we must make sure that Brendan knows that it is his duty to choose a best man and some ushers for the ceremony. I know who I would like to be the best man – Vincent, of course – but dear Brendan may have different ideas! Oh, I am beginning to get very apprehensive about the whole thing!"

"So long as it does not become a burden, my dear – remember that a beautiful wedding is a young girl's dream. I am taken back in memory to my own, and I realize that it is at times like this that I really miss your Papa most poignantly!" And Louise gathered her daughter in her arms, hugging and kissing her, with tears streaming down her cheeks.

Chapter 47

There was so much to do, so many arrangements to make, that four or five weeks flew by for all concerned. But then, about a week before the ceremony, came two events that confirmed for everyone that all of this was really going to happen – first the wedding rehearsal and secondly Brendan's bachelor party.

The castle chaplain, Father Francis, took the role of celebrant at the rehearsal, as Bishop Nathaniel of Hastings had agreed to conduct only the actual ceremony. Brendan had chosen an old friend from his youth, Lord Mortimer of Sevenoaks, to be his best man, and had selected two more as ushers from his circle of local friends. Despite Beatrice's disappointment, Vincent was not at all put out by being left out of these choices.

So the wedding party and all the bridesmaids were led through the various parts of the proceedings, save only for the giving and receiving of the rings. There were no real hitches, just some minor hesitations, notably when little Amelia, the smallest bridesmaid, was suddenly overcome by shyness in the middle of the saying of the vows and ran and hid herself in the vestry. Beatrice promised everyone that she would take Amelia aside and talk gently to her, to make sure that this did not happen on the day.

As for Brendan's bachelor party, nobody knew much about it, since he had invited only friends from earlier days; his best man, Lord Mortimer, of course, and a dozen other young men altogether, some that he had met at the two schools he had attended in his youth and even an acquaintance or two whom he had encountered roistering in local taverns during a short period when he had as an adolescent been trying this sort of activity out – half-heartedly it must be said.

He did ask Vincent to attend this party, more out of a sense of obligation rather than of inclination, but Vincent gracefully declined, not wanting to risk putting a damper on the proceedings. He felt that he and Brendan had eventually, after a shaky start, come to have relations that were cordial but not especially deep.

So, the day after the rehearsal with several days remaining before the wedding, Brendan ordered the chaise, at about eight o'clock in the evening, with Clive as driver, to take him to an inn in a small town on the road to Hastings, where the bachelor feast had been arranged. He had developed a consideration for others that had not always been evident in him in earlier years, and rather than having Clive the coachman wait, allowed him to return to the castle, bidding him to return to collect the groom and his best man, Mortimer, who was going to be staying at the castle, at between two and three o'clock of the next morning.

Louise, Beatrice and the others waved him off, telling him not to over-indulge, and giving him other familial exhortations, and then returned to their own activities. The dressmakers were going to be in attendance for a few days, Florence being the main centre of their activities as they, and the maids who were in charge of her makeup, made sure that the bride in her elaborate wedding gown would look as beautiful as possible on the day of the wedding. The bridesmaids, too, were receiving similar attention, albeit less concentrated.

All went to bed fairly early, including Vincent, who had been energetically active in a number of ways. At about four in the morning, however, he was woken abruptly once again by Clive, who apologized profusely, saying, "Mr Vincent, I seem to be doing this frequently, but I assure you, it is not for the same reason this time. I went to collect Lord Brendan at the inn, as he had instructed me. When I arrived, however, he was not there. A group of his friends were waiting for their own carriages, or for their horses to be prepared, as the case might be. They were all fairly jovial and cried out to me in recognition, saying 'Brendan and Mortimer are already gone – Brendan's grandmother came in her own carriage for them, not half an hour since.' Of course, Mr Vincent, I was astounded, knowing that neither of Lord Brendan's grandmothers were still alive – I knew Lady Louise's Mama well, until she passed away."

"So," said Vincent, "did you ask about this false grandmother?"

"Of course, Sir, but all they could tell me was that Brendan was rather befuddled with drink by that time and went with the woman with no demur. Lord Mortimer simply fell in with his friend, knowing no better, I suppose. I asked them to describe the woman and her coach, but they just said that she was an elderly grey-haired person, not very handsome, and that the coach was entirely black, and driven by a coachman who seemed to be well-wrapped against the cold, all dressed in furs."

"Oh!" exclaimed Vincent, "This woman's description sounds all too akin to that of someone we have heard about recently. I must talk to Lady Louise and Lady Beatrice about this with no delay. Thank you Clive, now please tell me where this inn is, and I will go and consult with the ladies."

"Well, Sir, it will be easy to find – it is in a village called Footscray, less than half an hour's drive from here on the Hastings road. The inn, on the left of the road in the middle of the village, is under the sign of the crossed keys. I can drive you there, of course, should you wish."

Vincent sent for a maid to see whether Louise and Beatrice were up and about yet. Being told that they were, he went to Louise's apartment where he found them in conversation.

"Forgive me, ladies, for interrupting, but there is new drama concerning Brendan!" And he went on to relate all that Clive had told him.

Louise instantly jumped to the same conclusion as he had, saying, "I somehow thought that we might not have heard the last of Lady Fafnirsdottir! But I believe that the incantation that Aggie's Auntie Ivy, Beatrice and I invoked will be effective in protecting any of we three from her malicious assaults. Beatrice, my love, do you think you could use your new-found seer's skills to locate Brendan for us?"

Beatrice closed her eyes and concentrated hard. After a few moments, her lips parted in a soft smile and she announced, "I have him! He appears to be lying on a cot in a small room, with his friend Mortimer by his side. Come, Mama and Vincent, let us dream travel there immediately!"

She started the humming, and soon they found themselves skimming above the trees of a dense forest. In a clearing, they could see a substantial stone-built house. They descended and manifested in the room that Beatrice had envisioned. There was Brendan, snoring on a cot, while Mortimer was apparently just rousing himself from where he had been lying on the floor.

Louise went over to her son and carefully grasped his arm. He woke with a start, and peered about him, rubbing his eyes with his fist. "Why, Mama!" he said, "What are you doing here? I was just about to set off home!" Looking around he asked, "But where are we?" And then he suddenly remembered the witch, crying, "What has she done to me now?"

Chapter 48

Brendan went on, "Oh, she must have enchanted me – I have a splitting headache and my mouth is dry!" Louise, in quiet tones, slightly amused, told him that it was no enchantment, but that he was simply suffering a hangover from the drink he had taken during the evening and night, and then explained that they had come there to confront Fafnirsdottir. She did not question Brendan any further, as it was obvious that he had been befuddled during the encounter with the witch, to the extent that he had gone with her without hesitation. She turned to Lord Mortimer, in the hope that he might remember more, since he appeared to be more alert than Brendan.

He thought for a moment and then said that he could picture the woman well, and also had a good sight of the coachman. "I took her to be Brendan's grandmother, as she had claimed, so I was interested to see what sort of a woman she might be. But to me she appeared just to be an elderly woman with long bedraggled grey hair, and sharp features, a little taller than Brendan, which made her above average height for a woman, but somewhat stooped. Her clothing was not elegant and she was untidy. As for the coachman, he was short and stout, but the chief feature of interest to me was that he was wrapped in thick furs, although the night was not very cold. And as for his hands – I saw with a shock that he appeared to have too many fingers! He spoke not, but merely helped the woman to bundle us into the coach. I went without protest, still believing her to be who she claimed."

Louise thanked him for giving such a clear account, saying, "That sounds very much like Fafnirsdottir to me – let us investigate further. I believe that Beatrice and I are safe from her influence after the rituals we went through the other day, but we shall still need to step carefully."

Vincent went over and tried the door, and, much to his surprise, found that it was not locked. He cautiously pulled it open a crack and peered out, then shut it quickly. "There are several wild wolves in the hall – she must have judged that they would provide a sufficient guard over us. But she has not taken into account that we are able to commune with these creatures! Let me speak with them."

He called out to them in wolf language, telling them that they had nothing to fear from him or his companions, and that, if necessary, he would take care of any trouble from their mistress. Then Vincent, seeing that the three wolves were now quietly lying in the hall, one of them even wagging his tail like a pet dog, opened the door fully and led his friends out from the room. The wolves made no move to confront them.

The hallway led to a pair of imposing doors, and they crept as silently as possible towards them. Then Louise looked around, stopped and gestured to the others to do likewise, saying, "This building does not look quite right to me – let us see." She made a sweeping gesture and intoned a phrase in a language that neither Beatrice nor Vincent could follow, with the astounding effect that the walls gradually became misty and soon the entire building vanished, leaving the five standing in the centre of a woodland grove. The wolves took the opportunity to run away through the trees.

Brendan and Mortimer, of course, were left gawping about them with their mouths open!

And then Beatrice exclaimed, "There she is!" and pointed towards a grassy tussock under a spreading tree, where the witch Fafnirsdottir was seated, looking very angry but not attempting to move or speak.

Louise said quietly to Beatrice and Vincent, "It is as I hoped – our ceremony the other day has counteracted her magical powers and even her ordinary facilities of movement and speech at any time when we are present, especially since there are two of us here together. She would be bound by the same effects were she to try to approach the purlieus of Aunt Ivy's cottage."

And out loud, she addressed the witch, "Lady Fafnirsdottir, if that truly be your name, take heed of what I say. I hereby command you to leave this land of England before midnight of this day. If you refuse, my friends and I will take such further action as will cause you the greatest astonishment – wherever you try to hide we shall be able to seek you out! You can already see that our powers of white witchcraft are superior to your own evil trickery. Begone, I say! I now release your tongue, that you may answer."

At a gesture from Louise, the witch began to rant, "You have me at your mercy now, Lady Louise de Gonville Musgrave, and

I am forced to obey you. But it will not always be thus, so I enjoin you not to forget me, nor to imagine that I have surrendered to you for all time. I will now call my coach and driver, that I might depart with some style, so do not hinder me further."

She clicked her long bony fingers, and the black coach appeared, with the troll driver on the box; he descended and took her to the steps of the coach and handed her in. With a roar like thunder, and in a cloud of smoke, the coach and its occupants vanished, leaving behind a patch of scorched turf and a smell of brimstone.

Louise and Beatrice embraced Brendan, while Vincent shook Mortimer's hand and thanked him for keeping his head, "You have shown yourself a reliable best man – but let us hope your services will not be called upon in this way until long after the ceremony!"

It was no more than a few minutes later that they were all back at the castle. The first thing that Beatrice said on arrival was, "My word, I am so famished! Let us see whether we can all be provided with a substantial meal without delay!"

And Louise asked the maids who brought the food and drink to the small dining room soon afterwards, to enquire of Mistress Travis whether she would be so kind as to send Aggie up to her. When the girl arrived, Louise told her that she could tell her Aunt Ivy, next time she visited her, that the enchantment they had cast together had proved to be very effective, "Please tell your aunt that none of us should be bothered by Fafnirsdottir for many a year now, thanks to her efforts. And thank you too, Aggie, for your help!"

Brendan and Mortimer were advised to rest for the remainder of the day, and to make sure they got a good night's sleep. "We wouldn't want you to fall asleep during the service, would we?" said Beatrice – and everyone laughed happily.

Louise, too, said that she felt in need of a rest as well, "Casting enchantments leaves me rather drained – I think I might be getting a little too old for all this magic!" To which remark, Beatrice and Vincent were quick to deny any signs of aging, Beatrice saying, "If anything, Mama, you become more youthful day by day – please put any thoughts of retirement aside!"

Chapter 49

Over the next day or two, the wedding guests started arriving at the castle, among them one or two welcome surprises. Louise had been a little doubtful of the propriety of inviting the King and Queen, given the earlier banishment of Brendan, so it was very pleasing that King Arnold and Queen Tabitha accepted readily, saying that it in any case it would be exceedingly awkward to ignore the wedding, taking place as it was in the same castle in which they were now resident, but that they certainly bore no animosity to Brendan and particularly none to Florence. Their Majesties took the couple aside and handed them the deeds to their wedding present, a village called Lesser Hythe, on the coast west of Hastings, which included a fine manor-house, an estate functioning well under a bailiff ever since the previous noble owners had both passed away leaving no heirs, and a fine old church of Norman architecture, with the new owners having the right to appoint a replacement vicar, should they choose to. The incumbent, said Tabitha, was an elderly person who tended to give the same sermon every week, so that the congregation was somewhat dwindling, but that he should certainly, because of his long service, be given a cottage and an endowment that would help him to see out his days.

And the Queen's sister, Lady Margarethe, arrived from her home in York, full of enthusiasm, also bringing with her a present – a beautiful pair of milk-white greyhounds. "I know not whether any other wedding gifts are on open display, but I could hardly parcel up these two splendid beasts – they are already house-trained and obedient, but will need to be trained in coursing if Brendan wishes them to be used that way. You may change the names as you wish, of course, but we have been calling them Castor and Pollux, and they answer immediately to these."

The parents of the bride, the Duke and Duchess of Dorset, drove up in their coach along with an additional carriage carrying a contingent of eight of their little nieces who would be bridesmaids, with a governess to keep them under control. As Duke Henry said, "We have had them visit us many times at home, and although they are very sweet children and we love them dearly, they are very hard to keep track of – there are two

145

sets of twins among them, and they take delight in causing confusion. Little girls in my youth seemed much more tractable than these children of today!" Duchess Elfrida added, "We have arranged for them to be dressed all alike for the service, in pale lilac shades – I hope that their dresses do not clash too much with Beatrice's!"

Beatrice was quick to allay her anxiety, saying, "No, no – my dress is of white and turquoise, so it will tone in quite well, I should think. As for keeping track of them, I have an idea or two that might help us there! I have been a wild little girl myself in my time, though you may not think it now!"

A special room had been set aside for the display of wedding gifts. It was guarded at all times by soldiers from the royal household, since there were many valuable items, including silverware carefully selected by Fritzi and Clotilda from the now extensive stocks of their three shops, and a beautiful bracket clock, wondered at by all who beheld it, since such clocks were a very modern embellishment to only the most progressive noble homes. This was a present from Graf Wilhelm von Wilderswil and the Grafine Sybilla, who sent their apologies for not being able to attend the wedding, since their Frankfurt establishment was becoming extraordinarily busy, writing, "And we owe our success largely to the efforts of your relatives and friends, so maybe this small gift may be regarded as a tribute to the Musgrave family at large, not merely to Lord Brendan and his bride, who we were pleased to meet when they visited Schloss Kirschbaum recently."

There was another notable gift, from Beatrice and Vincent together, a carriage in the most modern style, with the de Gonville-Musgrave arms emblazoned on the doors, together with a team of four jet-black horses.

Finally, Lady Louise gave the fortunate pair a gold locket each, with a miniature portrait of herself inside. But, as she explained to them, "These are not merely decorative baubles – they confer the gift of veracity to anyone wearing or holding them, and they are also enchanted so that they cannot be stolen!"

All the guests spent hours wandering at leisure about the room in which most of the gifts were displayed (save only the greyhounds and the carriage-and-four), and were duly admiring of them. There were, of course, many smaller gifts, including a ceremonial sword for Brendan and a very up-to-the minute porcelain coffee service for Florence, presented by Lord Mortimer, as well as jewellery and more mundane household items.

As new guests arrived, the gathering formed into groups and reformed again, chatting and exchanging histories, and, of course, playing cards and board games accompanied by refreshments and drinks. Guillaume du Boise, his family and his other musicians provided a soothing melodious background except when they were called upon to accompany lively dances. The weather had turned quite cold, so only the most energetic ventured outside, to take walks through the snow-covered gardens and the wider demesne. The entire atmosphere at the castle was cordial and optimistic, and every time the prospective bride and groom were met by a new guest, they were deluged with congratulations and good wishes.

The company had been promised what Mistress Travis referred to as "modest suppers" on the two nights before the wedding – but what she called modest would have been judged extravagant banquets in many another noble household. The guests, in general, took that description to mean that they could wander in and out of the dining hall as they pleased, taking snacks as and when fancy demanded, and then returning to whatever pursuit they were immersed in.

So, one way and another, the evening's entertainment, as well as being mightily enjoyable was quite protracted – certain guests, notably those ladies most enthusiastic for card-playing, were very late in taking to their beds, while some gentlemen, let it be said, had to be aroused by the servants from where they had been snoring on couches in corners here and there, and persuaded to go to their rooms.

Lady Hermione, feeling that she was still on duty as a chaperone, fussed about, sending Florence off to bed early, saying, "Now try not to think of tomorrow too much, dear!" – which, of course only made her more nervous. Hermione took a different line with Brendan, exhorting him to have a long conversation with his Mama before also having an early night, but not saying anything about his possible apprehensiveness. "He is a man, after all," she told herself, "and men don't concern themselves with their feelings as much as we women. What a pity Brendan's Papa is no longer with us. A boy really needs his father's counsel at a time like this."

Chapter 50

The morning of the wedding day dawned to find many of those at the castle already up and about. In one large room, all the little bridesmaids were being dressed and having their hair done, amid outbursts of giggling and an occasional squeal as a nursemaid pulled too hard while twining flowers into a little girl's hair.

Louise, Beatrice and several of the other adults had opted to have breakfast brought to their chambers so that they could dress without too much rush. Beatrice had decided to try the new fashion of having her nails treated with scented red oil and buffed to a high polish with a chamois leather cloth – she had brought in a young woman from the town who was adept in this art. And all the ladies, including the bride herself, were submitting to the attentions of maids who were applying their makeup and adjusting the powdered wigs of those ladies who were more mature and preferred to wear them rather than their own hair.

Even Brendan had been persuaded to pay more attention to his own appearance than he was accustomed to admit – he had declined to wear a wig but had agreed to having his hair pomaded and curled.

All this activity was suspended when it was announced that the Bishop of Hastings was arriving in his white coach accompanied by a retinue of minor clerics. Lady Louise and the Duke and Duchess of Dorset greeted the Bishop at the castle entrance, whereupon the bishop ushered one of the clergy forward, saying, "I think you may remember Cyril Cornhill, the Rector of St. Anthony's, Dunton Green!" It was, of course, the young priest who had intervened with the runaway pair – he was thanked effusively, particularly by the Duchess.

The entourage was then led to a waiting room that had been specially prepared, with a selection of refreshments already set out for the Bishop and his staff.

And before very long it was time for the ceremony. All went to plan – Florence's father led the bride to join Brendan at the altar at the appropriate moment, none of the little bridesmaids misbehaved or forgot what to do, and the happy pair spoke their lines perfectly. The whole of the proceedings was enhanced by the selections played by the musicians, and finally Master Arbutius directed the choir in leading the bridal party in procession out of the chapel, while they sang an anthem in their sweet young voices.

Everyone milled about, chatting enthusiastically about the success of the celebrations, and then they all drifted happily into the grand dining hall for the wedding feast and the speeches.

Within two days of the ceremony, almost all the guests had taken their leave, so the remaining residents of the castle began to feel rather lonely.

Beatrice, especially, described her emotions to her mother, "Well, Mama, we must admit, finally, that my birthday celebrations have truly come to an end. But, strangely, although before the wedding I had begun to feel rather distressed at the passing of time, I am now in a quite tranquil frame of mind and find that I am looking forward, not back."

Louise hugged her daughter, saying, "I am relieved for you, my dear. I was a little concerned before, but I see now that you have come to terms with the inevitable. But what, tell me, are your plans for the future? Have you any projects in mind? Are there any duties to do with the castle you wish to take over from me, for example?"

"Well, Mama, I was thinking rather of what I might do with Bramwell Hall and its estates. I do not wish to reside there, but I would like to see it developed, either by the present tenants or others we might find. Today the park is hardly more than a series of fields – it badly wants the services of a skilled landscape designer. Do you know of any, Mama?"

"No, I can't say I do, but maybe our estimable builder, Mr Hutchinson, would be a good person to ask. I know he has worked on several manor houses and estates beside this castle. He has high standards himself and would not, I believe, recommend any but those with assured competence and highest tastes. And I think that you should also consult Vincent – he has a wealth of knowledge and experience."

"Oh, Mama," cried Beatrice, "I would never embark on any enterprise without speaking to him! He is my dearest friend, as you know."

Louise saw to her surprise that tears had come to her daughter's eyes. "Why, my dear, whatever is the matter?"

"I suppose that the wedding of Florence and Brendan has made me take on a sentimental mood – I keep thinking that Vincent and I are already as suited to become a loving married couple as anyone else that I know – but, Mama, it would not be proper for me to raise the subject with him, would it?"

Louise hugged her daughter, saying, "Beatrice, my dear one, am I really hearing you aright? How can I believe that you, who have been so assertive, even forceful, on so many occasions in the past, are capable of quailing at that prospect? Go ahead – propose to him today, for goodness' sake – or would you rather wait for a leap year?"

At that, Beatrice stood up, shook herself, kissed her mother and strode out of the room, headed for the gardens, where she knew she would find Vincent tending to his bees.

And, at dinner that evening, Vincent stood up and made this announcement: "Your Majesties, Lady Louise de Gonville Musgrave and all here present, I have this afternoon asked Lady Beatrice for her hand in marriage, and, to my inexpressible joy, she has consented to become my wife. I know not when the wedding will be, but I hope it will be soon."

He gathered Beatrice up in his arms and they kissed long and intensely, to the acclamation of everyone around the table.

King Arnold was the first to offer his congratulations, wishing them well, but adding a reservation, "Of course, Beatrice and Vincent will want a proper honeymoon, and there are still arrangements to be made before they can be wed, but I wish to make a claim on each of them. I trust that they will find it possible for both of them to serve me as my principal advisers, since they have complementary skills and capabilities. It will make Queen Tabitha and me very happy if they are prepared to agree to such an arrangement. Please say you will, Beatrice and Vincent!" And, of course, they did so, gladly, coming and kneeling before their majesties, who embraced them and shook their hands accordingly.

And so it was that a new episode began in the lives of Lady Beatrice de Gonville Musgrave and Vincent Crabbe, of Woodhampton Castle.

FINIS

www.ingramcontent.com/pod-product-compliance
Lightning Source LLC
Chambersburg PA
CBHW051835170626
46807CB00003B/1188